Step Lightly

Kendall Klym

Livingston Press
The University of West Alabama

Hardcover binding by: HF Group
Typesetting and page layout: Sarah Coffey
Proofreading: Jashaunda Allen, Barbara Anderson, Jenna Frye,
Jayla Gellington, Layla Lewis, Shameika McKinstry,
Joy Richardson, Joe Taylor, Erin Watt.
Cover layout: Joe Taylor
Cover Painting: Ken Southwick

Step Lightly

Kendall Klym

For my parents,

Nicholas and Lillian Klym

A number of people have offered inspiration and help that enabled me to complete this manuscript. I thank the late Richard M. Sirota, Nicholas and Lillian Klym, Joe Taylor, Christina Consolino, Ruth Sirota, Jenny Sadre-Orafai, Katherine Hyon, Melissa Keith, Andy Plattner, Jessica Watson, H. William Rice, Joan Kunsch, Claire Leatham, Harold Raynor, the late Edith Raynor, Ken Southwick, Richard Raynor, Silvia Kofler, Louise Runyon, Pamela Mencher, Tom Yzaguirre, Kim Shope, Dirk van der Linde, Bobbi Dickinson, Dominica Dipio, Laura Davis, the late Julia Markham, the late Stella Walter, the late Claudette Smith, Beth Giddens, Jem Poster, JoAnn LoVerde-Dropp, Carol Morris, the late J.M. Barrie, Martin and Eugenia Lanaux, Mikhail Baryshnikov, the late Anna Pavlova, Leslie Choron, the late Fred Astaire, the late Ginger Rogers, the late Italo Calvino, the late Martha Graham, the late Carol Shields, the late Mark Twain, the late Charlotte Perkins Gilman, the late Willa Cather, and the late George Balanchine.

I think the reason dance has held such an ageless magic for the world is that it has been the symbol of the performance of living. . . . The instrument through which the dance speaks is also the instrument through which life is lived—the human body. . . . It holds in its memory all matters of life and death and love. . . . Movement never lies. It is a barometer telling the state of the soul's weather to all who can read it. This might be called the law of the dancer's life.

–Martha Graham

Acknowledgments

"A Professional Male Ballet Dancer in Twelve Steps," second-prize winner of the *Baltimore Review* Short Story Contest, first appeared in the Winter 2017 issue of the *Baltimore Review*.

"Come Dance with Me" first appeared in *Fiction International*, World in Pain issue, 2018.

"Marva and Misha" first appeared in *Best Short Stories from the Saturday Evening Post Great American Fiction Contest 2015*.

"Origin" first appeared in the Spring 2016 issue of *Thorny Locust*.

"Pavlova," runner-up winner of the Howard Frank Mosher Fiction Prize, first appeared in the Winter 2013 issue of *Hunger Mountain*.

"Poisoning the Dick" first appeared in *pacificREVIEW*, States of La Frontera issue, 2018.

"The Ballet Class" first appeared in the May 2012 issue of the *Bryant Literary Review*.

"The Belly Dance" first appeared in the Summer 2017 issue of the *Tampa Review*.

"The Continental" first appeared in *Best Short Stories from the Saturday Evening Post Great American Fiction Contest 2014*, and then in the Spring 2014 issue of *The Broad River Review*.

"The Dance Quiz" first appeared in *Articulated Short Story Anthology* 2016.

"The Dancing Bee" first appeared in *The Chattahoochee Review*, vol. 34, no. 2.

"The Dancing Plague," first-prize winner in the *Puerto del Sol* Fiction Contest 2013, first appeared in *Puerto del Sol*, vol. 49., no. 1.

"The Nebraska Hula," a semifinalist in *The Tishman Review* Fiction Contest, first appeared in the January 2018 edition of *The Tishman Review*.

"Tinker Bell Laundry Detergent" first appeared in the inaugural edition of *Curating Alexandria*, 2018.

Contents

Introduction

Before I ever took ballet lessons or read a book of fiction, I made my first connection between stories and dance. I couldn't have been more than 3, when a landscape painting caught my attention. Hanging on the wall of the living room, the painting featured a row of deciduous trees flanking a woodland trail, yellow and red leaves forming a mosaic in the middle of the path. That was the place I wanted to be. Why, I'm not exactly sure, but I know it had something to do with loneliness. I recall the dull ache that still revisits my bones, muscles, and organs whenever I feel isolated and misunderstood.

Planning how I would access that trail distracted me from feeling so lonely. I knew I couldn't walk into the artwork, especially after I was told not to touch it, so I began to conduct experiments. If I turned around in circles as fast as I could, it looked like the painting was moving. If the painting and I were both moving, I believed I could move into the painting. When my experiment failed, I refused to give up. I distinctly remember counting the number of steps it took to complete a revolution. Knowing the right number was important. Getting the right footing was also important. While practicing, I visualized what I would do once I gained entry: head down the path, past the part where the frame cut off the scene. Once I was out of sight, I would meet a friend, talk to the woodland animals. We would all run and jump and play. We would have a wonderful time. This fragment of a story, which continues to stand prominently in my mind, accompanied me as I danced around in circles. The more I practiced, the faster I became. Gaining momentum and speed, I was on the verge of entering another world.

Although I never really entered the painting, I accomplished two important tasks: dancing and creating a story. I guess I've always wanted to do both, despite warnings that I would have to choose one art form over the other. Fortunately, those warnings did not come from my parents, who encouraged me to pursue what I loved, and I did, thanks to their help. At 15, when I was accepted into the prestigious School of American Ballet, my father drove me four days a week from West Hartford, Connecticut, to New York City for pre-professional training. That was the same year I learned about gerunds, participial phrases, and nominative absolutes, elements of grammar that beckoned me to see how they work, to write. If asked which I preferred—dancing or writing—I would have refused to make a decision.

When friends and family found out that my 52-year-old father was driving me 250 miles a day after putting in a full day of work as a high school teacher, they said the stunt was crazy, the car would break down, and I would fail 9th grade. Stubborn and determined, my parents and I worked together. My mother, who awakened at 5 a.m. to get ready for work, had dinner ready at 10:30 p.m., when we finally returned home. Considering my parents had failed to predict one of New York's infamous transit strikes, which increased the commute to three hours each way, the naysayers had their point. However, I was never late for any class, I excelled in ballet, and I earned A's in all academic subjects, achieving a rank of first in my class by the end of the school year. In the car I did homework, using a makeshift light my father designed to plug into the cigarette lighter after dark. When we were stuck at a stoplight, Dad helped me with math, drawing equations in the condensation on the windshield. For English, I wrote about my dance experiences, and when I danced, I allowed my body to release the burgeoning anger and frustration I felt for being different, for choosing ballet instead of sports, for being called *weird* by other children, and *spoiled* by their adult counterparts.

As I think about the choices my parents and I made, about the poverty-line salaries I earned as a professional ballet dancer, about the general lack of understanding and acceptance so many Americans have expressed toward the arts and creativity, I know exactly why I chose to be a dancer and a writer: to make up for being unheard and misunderstood. Combine words and movement in just the right way, and you can get people to listen and feel. You can chip away at the laziness that feeds prejudice and bigotry—narrow-mindedness that causes a person to classify a professional ballet dancer as unimportant, as compared to a medical doctor. You can even keep from feeling lonely.

My goal in this collection is to use words and stories to redefine dance—to show that we all dance, whether we are performing a ballet or an appendectomy. Perhaps the surgeon who removed your appendix never had the privilege of studying ballet, but the movements she made when slicing into your abdomen require the precision and artistry of a ballet dancer raising his partner in a bluebird lift, making sure she looks beautiful and stays safe. Both sets of hands manipulate bodies. Both the dancer and the doctor set out to improve and preserve humans' quality of life. When such a comparison is made, the definition of dance expands. My stories redefine dance through characters who run the gamut, from professional ballet dancers and directors in "Pavlova" to honeybees and a piano teacher in "The Dancing Bee." While the collection focuses more on ballet than other dance forms, common themes predominate, including the loss of love and the devastation of war. My hope is that through these stories readers can make their own connection between language and dance, and that they can add to my definition of dance.

Many have argued that the beauty of ballet lies in the fact that dance is an art form that transcends words, and any attempt to use words to describe dance would be in vain. That argument overlooks the accessibility of dance. I believe it is a misconception that ballet and other dance forms are effete, indescribable, and stuffy, that they are meant for only a select few who have nothing better to do than support classism and flaunt their wealth. The protagonist in "The Continental" holds such a misconception. But when he attends to his sick wife, his attitude changes. When he learns of his wife's last wish before she dies, he discovers a most unusual relationship between words and dance.

Unfortunately, very few in the real world become so enlightened. Dance supporters, alongside those who couldn't care less about dance or any other performing art, often fail to allow language and dance to coalesce. I remember sitting in the halls of the School of American Ballet reading a textbook while waiting for the studio doors to open, when Lincoln Kirstein, the legendary founder of the New York City Ballet, walked by dressed in a black suit, his towering shadow darkening the words on the page I was reading. A colleague told me that Kirstein wanted to see the dancers stretching, not reading. The next time the behemoth made his rounds, I performed a perfect side split, placing my open book between my legs. No one, including the great Kirstein, was going to impede my relationship with words and dance.

My linguistic aptitude did little to endear me to dance colleagues and superiors; however, my developing relationship with language and dance led to my greatest success as a professional dancer: I was on tour in St. Louis performing the role of the Nutcracker Soldier Doll for a group of school kids at 8 a.m., having finished a show at 11 p.m. the previous night. After the morning performance, I was ordered to go out front in costume and socialize with the children. I can just imagine the look on my face when I set foot into the house. Youngsters, in my eyes, were the enemy—the undisciplined idiots who tortured me for years because I studied ballet. It didn't matter that these were children brought to the ballet by educators. Old memories had clouded my judgment. But with painted wooden sword at my side, I followed directions.

I will never forget the reward I received. A boy in a wheelchair, 13 or 14 years old, reached out with his hand and stopped me. "You were so good," he said. "I felt your dance. I was up there with you." While the encounter lasted a matter of seconds, I have thought about it for years. The boy made me feel like a hero—not because I represented good conquering evil, part of the handsome Nutcracker army that defeats the ugly Mouse King and his misshapen army of mice, but because my dancing had a healing effect. I caused the boy to feel something, when medical professionals may have given up on him, when he may have been told by experts he would never feel anything, certainly not in his legs. I can only imagine what the boy felt, since I, along with most people, have the privilege of being able to walk. The memory of the encounter makes me thankful for my own abilities, both as a dancer and as a writer able to share my experience.

This scenario gets me thinking about dance, not only as a form of entertainment, but also as a method of communication, a text so to speak. Have you ever seen Prince Florimund declare his love for Princess Aurora, after the kiss, in the ballet *Sleeping Beauty*? He extends his left arm toward the princess, steps back, and places his right hand on his chest. Then he gathers both hands at his heart and points to his ring finger. These movements are a form of text that the audience reads. Whether you're sitting in the front row or the second balcony, you know exactly what is happening. You feel the romance and excitement as a result of text performed through the art of dance.

Decades after the termination of my dance career, I attribute my roles in ballets such as *Sleeping Beauty* and *The Nutcracker*, alongside my encounter with the disabled boy, as an impetus to use words to convey the importance of dance to the world. Since so few people experience the beauty of professional dance, I know that the stage is not my venue. Fiction, on the other hand, reaches people of all backgrounds and abilities. Reading is a way of accomplishing the impossible, of entering a painting and creating our own stories in the midst of someone else's. Writing is my way of conveying what it's like to dance. I use my imagination to express a feeling—a movement that becomes alive in the reader's imagination, enabling that person to experience that feeling. Through the literary device of synesthesia—a sensation in one section of the body produced by stimulation of another section—I can tell readers that leaping high in the air and landing with soft precision feels like a seagull sounds when it calls out and then dives into the ocean to catch a fish.

Dance is something we all do, whether we know it or not. Climbers, when they rappel into the Grand Canyon, use the same techniques dancers use to land gracefully from a jump. Lovers perform a dance when their bodies merge. Words dance. Language is the choreography that joins reader to writer in a dance that obscures the distinction between human and text, the dancer and the dance. Consider how William Butler Yeats ends his poem "Among School Children": "O body swayed to music, O brightening glance/ How can we know the dancer from the dance?" You, the reader, have your own life, your memories and imagination, which become intertwined with my life, my memories and imagination, through the fiction I write. Through our interactions with text, we become both the dancer and the dance. The ambiguity rendered from the dancer becoming enmeshed with the dance reflects a complex and dynamic relationship. According to feminist philosopher Elizabeth Grosz, the "body and the modes of sensual perception which take place through [the body] are not mere physical/physiological phenomena; nor are they simply psychological results of physical causes. Rather they affirm the necessary connectedness of consciousness as it is incarnated." Is it possible that when we read, we turn consciousness into a physical being, not completely our own, but part of other physical beings, people with whom we begin to connect? In his novel *Howard's End,* E.M. Forster appears to address such a connection between Margaret and Mr. Wilcox in the following statement: "Mature as he was, she might yet be able to help him to the building of the rainbow bridge that should connect the prose in us with the passion."

What is the "prose in us?" What does it look like, and how does it feel? I see the collective or shared prose between you and me, reader and writer, as a collection of dance stories, *pas des deux,* in which we enter the stage for an introductory dance, separate to perform our solos, and then join once again in a finale. As you read my words, we establish an initial connection; the dance is intimate yet subtle and tentative. We're just getting to know each other through the first impression of a character, the introduction of a scene. Then, as I express my words on paper or screen, I perform my solo. As you interpret my words, you have your solo. As my unwritten stories, personal and internal, blend with the fiction I write, interacting with your stories, personal and internal, we dance once again. This is our finale, in which consciousness incarnates: the prose connects with the passion, the reader becomes the writer, and the dancer becomes the dance.

Dance has certainly placed me outside the mainstream, yet the most important benefit I glean from immersing myself in such an intense and mysterious art form is the desire to persevere. Thanks to the unprecedented physical and mental strenuousness of ballet, I have beaten the odds on many occasions. When I dance, my negative qualities—widespread irritability and a general lack of practicality—melt away through movement. When I write, I dance. But unlike the stage, which is unforgiving to dancers who mess up, texts can be revised and reworked many times before an audience reads them. As a perfectionist, I find this element of writing, the ability "to perfect the dance," the most compelling. If one were to ask me why I write and why I dance, I would give the same answer: to create and share worlds that encourage people to show respect for what is different, to have fun, and to connect.

As a creative writer and former professional ballet dancer, I believe that writing and reading fiction are a form of dance. Every time I create a story I imagine performing a *pas de deux* with each of my readers, partnering her or him through conflict, lifting that person into a world both foreign and familiar. The dance is sensual yet respectful. You are my partner. As I lead, I transmit words from my body to yours, text traversing the lobes of our brains, imagined lives entering the marrow of our bones, the movement we make inspiring a connection between us—a simple touch that sparks a memory, or, perhaps something more. If I reach you in a significant way, that touch will be imbedded in your body, called up when you go about your daily life and come across something that reminds you of our dance.

The Ballet Class

I'll be the first to admit that I'm no expert. I didn't start classes till I was 40, and my boobs go flying when I try to pirouette. But there's one thing I can tell you with confidence: despite his lack of coordination, Thom was a dancer. When it came to combinations, you were lucky to get two steps, maybe three, from the six-foot, good-natured lunk. After two years of beginner ballet, he could do a *glissade assemblé,* and that was with great trepidation. Sometimes, when he performed this simple set of steps, he looked as if he were suffering from Parkinson's, pausing with intensity between the glide and the jump. Yet there was something about him you could almost call graceful, especially when he was partnering. You always knew he cared, that he honored women, no matter who or how old they were. You could feel it in his touch. That's what made him graceful: his graciousness, his respect.

Thom was the only guy in the class, quite the underachiever at 16, but everybody liked him, and we all knew you didn't come to Midtown School of Ballet to pursue a career. People of all ages were put in the same class, and all levels were pretty much for beginners. But unlike some studios, especially those with names like Miss Deedle's and Allentino Academy of Artistic Expression, this place was legit. All the teachers were professionals. One came from the former USSR, said the Kansas wheatfields reminded her of her childhood in Ukraine. Old-fashioned but sweet, she carried a wooden pointer to touch body parts that failed to follow the rules. We all loved her. Davin, the short guy who taught Thom, a bunch of preteen girls, and a smattering of us middle-aged women, was just as nice. He never yelled or made catty remarks. He just taught.

Despite the convenient location and positive atmosphere, the studio setup was less than ideal. *Tombé pas de bourée glissade assemblé,* and you hit the wall. After a while, though, you got used to the small space: some chairs and a couch for the waiting area, a nice springy floor, and one bathroom with a broken lock. That's how I caught an accidental peek at Davin, nude, his left foot reaching into a dance belt. Nothing like that of a gym rat, his body was muscled but compact. It reminded me of an urban, small-space bedroom—you know, with a teakwood desk and attached bookcase, bed overhead: so stylishly understated, perfectly balanced, every piece in place. From calves to forearms, he was covered in a veneer of slender musculature—his abdominals like rungs of a ladder that led to a firm but cozy bunk. When I gasped, Davin just laughed. After a moment, so did I. We had nothing to hide. Attraction was part of the business—one-sided or not.

But as amateur as we were, all except the teachers, everyone knew the Golden Rule of Ballet: to save it—the emotions, sex, whatever—for the audience. It didn't matter that the few who bothered to come in and sit down on the ripped Naugahyde were bored husbands, hyperactive children, and polite friends, more interested in talking on cell phones, playing computer games, or reading magazines than looking at us hopping around on *demi-pointe*. But that's what made it exciting: my husband, Emily's kids, the whole lot of them getting a jolt, a spark of electricity that stirred them out of their complacency.

* * *

One of the dancers—salt-and-pepper hair and a half-decent body—took ballet to even greater heights, or so she thought. Her name was Lisle. A former intern who got booted from residency for condemning abortions in the OR, she used to arrive early, say a prayer, and slip in a CD of Tchaikovsky or Debussy. Her lips curling with a look of either constipation or ecstasy, she waltzed around the studio, sometimes with a Bible in hand, dipping from side to side as if she were using the book to anoint the room. Then, about ten minutes before class started, she went to the toilet. One time, when I didn't have the car and Frank dropped me off early, Lisle asked me to the movies. They were showing *Black Swan* at the Megaplex, and she was organizing a protest.

"Hollywood's trying to desecrate the sacredness of ballet," she said, describing the film in graphic detail. "All about the flesh and damnation of the spirit."

"I'm not religious," I told her.

"But don't you believe in the sanctity of dance?"

She handed me a copy of John Paul II's *Letter to Artists*. I read a few lines: "Every genuine artistic institution goes beyond what the senses perceive and, reaching beneath reality's surface, strives to interpret its hidden mystery."

The former pope had a point. Whatever we had at Midtown, it certainly went beyond *my* senses, *my* reality. Davin's classes kept me young, gave me an edge. Ballet was something I took with me wherever I went, including the bedroom. Sex was never better. And when it came to Frank, who'd slept beside me for too many years, *that* was a miracle.

I said no to the protest. Sure, *Black Swan* was awful, and anybody who's ever done a *plié* knows that Natalie Portman can't dance, but at least someone took an interest in ballet, even if it was twisted and sick.

"It's the age we live in," I told Lisle. "Ballet went out when Baryshnikov got old. Society's into raunch and exhibitionism, not *Swan Lake*. The fact that a ballet movie even made it into the mainstream, never mind becoming a box-office hit, is astounding. Gotta take what you can get."

One day, when we were warming up before class, Lisle invited me to church.

"Before you say no," she said, "just hear me out."

She told me about some novice liturgical dancer coming to the cathedral. "I know you'll just love her performance."

"I'm confused," I said, looking Lisle square in the eye. "I thought Catholics weren't supposed to proselytize."

Thom, who was trying to put his head to his knee while keeping his foot latched to the bottom rung of the ballet barre, said he might go. When Lisle went to the toilet, we both started to laugh.

* * *

It's amazing how we all got along in those Thursday night classes—such different people, all lobbed together in

10

a less-than-adequate space. During the winter months, we'd gather by the steaming steel radiator to warm up. Sometimes we did Davin's "Squiggle Stretch." All you do is stand in parallel and squeeze your armpits closed while placing your hands in prayer position. Then, without letting your butt move an inch, you shimmy. Davin said the stretch stimulates the backbone, keeps it from freezing, when you have to hold yourself up. Thom said it makes you anal-retentive.

Despite all the joking around, when class started, everybody got serious. No talking allowed, unless there was a question, and even then, you had to raise your hand. A former soloist, Davin always upheld the dancer's tradition of discipline, but not with all the attitude and self-importance. A native Kansan, Davin trained in New York, spent a decade dancing in Denmark, and came home to attend college and teach. When giving corrections, Davin never touched below the shoulder or above the knee.

"Feel the butt come into the chest," he'd say, when we were all squiggling around unintentionally, trying to balance in *passé.* "Press down on your shoulders while pulling up on your lower body. Make the pressure equal—up to down, right to left. Then you can balance. Then you go nowhere."

And he was right, all except for the final statement. The few times I managed to stay in one spot without shaking or losing my balance, I knew I was on my way. If I balanced long enough, I went to the most amazing places: dense forests, high cliffs, endless sea. Once, when I lasted thirty seconds on high *relevé,* I felt as if I had morphed into a lighthouse, solid and staid, my blinking eyes warning ships of rocks below. The longer I remained steadfast, the more vessels I could rescue from ruin on the jagged Nova Scotia coast. Nothing, including sex, gave me more satisfaction than a long balance. Once I got my equilibrium, I felt timeless, standing there, high on the ball of the foot.

We each had our fantasies when it came to ballet. Thom wanted to fly. And every now and then, when you saw him jump, he did. Now I don't mean that he out-jumped Nureyev or Bujones or Baryshnikov. Most of the time, Thom's jumps were average at best. His Achilles' wasn't particularly long like Davin's, but if he took advantage of what little *plié* he had, he really took off. One night, when we were doing *glissade assemblé,* Davin told Thom to forget he was human, to assume the body of a bird.

"Swoop and then lift," said Davin, lowering and raising his arms in *écarté.*

Thom followed with an aerial assemblage of the legs that reminded me of a Kansas scissortail pursuing a fly. Lisle said he looked like an angel, led by St. Michael.

Davin said: "Good. Now do it again."

Thom couldn't.

Another time, when we gathered by the radiator, Thom said his best jumps came when he forgot about ballet, when he thought of something else.

I asked him what.

"Getting chased by a Pflugerblip."

Davin said he was crazy.

"Haven't you ever played Alien Awesome?" retorted Thom.

We hadn't.

After class, Thom took out his laptop and showed us a Pflugerblip. My first reaction was to laugh. But the longer I observed the purple blob rolling across the computer screen, squirting its victims and devouring their bodies, I told him I understood. Then I turned away.

* * *

Originally, Thom came to class because his girlfriend dragged him. Her name was Smyrna, and she quit after a month. No discipline. I guess she expected him to quit, too, and when he didn't, they broke up. She wasn't nice. After Davin started teaching adagio, Thom's body filled out. With seven females, that kid had his hands full—literally. And boy, did his muscles develop. From promenades to lifts, we worked him hard. Then we worked on Davin to get him to teach us the flying fish.

Breathing with her partner, the woman rises to the man's shoulders, enjoys an eagle's view, and then plunges to the floor, one leg in the air and the other wrapped around her partner's back. The man's hands go just about everywhere, from waist to chest to inner thigh.

As partners, Thom and Lisle were perfect for each other. Her head reached his face when she went *en pointe,* and they both had a similar bone structure. When they got their acts together, they looked good. Near the end of a class I won't forget, Thom nearly dropped Lisle. We were working on the fish, and instead of listening to corrections, Lisle was all over the place, flip-flopping like a fish on a line.

"Head up," said Davin, but to no avail.

When Thom lowered her, Lisle buckled in the middle. Luckily, she was smart enough to catch herself with her hands; otherwise, her head would have crashed to the floor. Her weight all in the wrong place, she slid through Thom's grip and landed on the linoleum, like a bag of Goldfish Crackers, tipping and dropping to the bottom of a vending machine.

"Sorry," said Lisle.

"Sorry," said Thom.

"Sorry's not going to do it," said Davin, "especially if somebody gets hurt. It's up to the woman to arch her back and keep it arched." He turned to Lisle. "He can't do it for you. The man can only go so far, especially when he's leaning forward. Gravity's in the way, which is why you've got to take charge of your own backbone. The woman works just as hard as the man—harder, if you take into account that she has to look like she's making no effort."

Lisle bit her lip. "This is harder than I thought."

"Let's try it again," said Thom.

"Wait a second," said Davin. "Lisle's not the only one at fault." He faced Thom. "Don't hold her close enough, and you lose her. The woman gets injured, and you get blamed, no matter what. That's how it works in ballet."

Davin demonstrated with me. Perched, suspended, and hovering: it was all over in a few seconds. The experience caused me to vibrate—not on the outside, but in my bones. Our bodies were one, Davin's breath breathing into mine, my strength an extension of his confidence. It was magnificent: two people touching intimately without the sex, a spiritual connection that can only come from contact that's physical. The movement was like a prayer.

Unfortunately, Thom and Lisle were too inhibited to experience the sanctity of sensuality. They failed to understand the importance of proximity. As the man switches his arms, the essence of friction is what makes it all work, especially in that single moment, when the man lets go, when the woman is airborne with no one holding on. As long as they stay connected with the breath, with the energy that dances between two bodies, the partners stay together. I felt it with Davin. Instead of getting that sinking sensation that I was about to fall, I experienced the opposite, as my chin dipped down to just a few inches above the floor. It was as if I were rising up, full and yeasty, like bread in the oven.

Smyrna, on the other hand, was more like a loaf that fell—a dumpy, bleached blond with a flat chest and cakey thighs. During the month she spent at Midtown, the only thing I ever heard her say was that Davin was gay, again and again, as if a gay ballet dancer were something novel, something worth alerting the media. I held my tongue, but several of the preteens told her to keep quiet. When she left, I thought we were rid of her. But out of the blue, at least a year after the breakup, Smyrna started showing up in the middle of adagio. From the doorway, she'd glare at Thom and whatever girl he was dancing with. When Thom ignored her, she'd leave. One time she sat down on the couch and wrote text messages, causing Thom's phone to bleat out a few bars of Aaron Copland's "Hoedown." We all laughed because Davin imitated the announcer in a television commercial that made the song popular: "Beef: it's what's for dinner." After that incident, Thom kept his phone turned off. Kimberly, the owner of the studio, banned Smyrna from the premises and made us lock the doors during class. That's how we lost our audience. The husbands, mothers, and friends waited in the car.

On a cold October evening, while waiting for our rides, Thom and I had a short conversation. His mother and my husband were late, and we had to stand outside once Kimberly closed the studio.

"So why do you dance?" I asked Thom.

"I don't know. Ballet gives me confidence."

14

Before I could address the issue, Thom asked me the same question. I told him ballet got me through the day, especially when my nerves were rattled.

"Same here," said Thom. "School gets on my nerves, and I think of Davin's class."

"What do the other kids think of your dancing?"

Thom's mother showed up before he could answer.

* * *

Last February, when the temperature hit 60, Kimberly left the door open to air out the studio. No one saw Smyrna come in, and she kept herself hidden for hours. Of course the only place she could have gone was the bathroom, behind the shower curtain of a tub that didn't work. There Smyrna stayed during technique class, a short break, and the first half of adagio. During the break, I didn't see the girl, but I definitely smelled her. The odor wasn't foul or perfumy, just different. Dance with a group for long enough, and your nose gets accustomed to each person's odor, no matter how slight or heavy. We sweated, which means we each had our own smell. Davin, for example, had a familiar odor—kind of like popcorn, when it just begins to inflate. During adagio, we mixed up our smells to form new smells. To me, we all smelled of movement and music—different scents chiming in as bodies assumed their appropriate places. Smyrna, on the other hand, smelled sedentary, sort of like old pizza that gets forgotten at the back of the refrigerator, not yet inedible, but definitely stale.

When Thom and Lisle attempted the flying fish, Smyrna emerged. Exiting the bathroom, she popped a piece of purple bubblegum into her mouth, tossing the wrapper on the floor. All I could think of was a Pflugerblip. Smyrna and I locked eyes— everyone else was ensconced with Thom, Lisle, and the fish— and she ambled over to the couch, cell phone in hand. Thom didn't see her.

It took only a moment for Lisle to waver on Thom's shoulder.

"Just bring her down," said Davin. "Don't do the fish. Her butt's not far back enough."

Thom agreed, but Lisle protested.

In a spastic move that somewhat resembled a squiggle stretch, Lisle lifted her chest and stuck out her butt. She was okay until she spotted Smyrna. Then her whole body hiccupped, her backbone buckling, her head flying toward the floor. Several of us gasped, and Davin, who was spotting the lift, lurched forward. The only way I can describe what happened next is that Thom, for less than a split second, lost his lack of coordination. Instead of letting Lisle fall from his grip, he bent his knees, stuck out his butt, and caught his partner's upper body. Lisle was safe. They didn't even need Davin. We all applauded—all except Smyrna, who snapped a picture, just at the moment of impact, just as Thom's right arm reached over Lisle's breasts.

"You can let go now," said Lisle, somewhat grateful.

Thom released his partner and started to go after Smyrna. "Give me that cell phone."

"Don't bother," I said. "She's not worth it. Don't give her the satisfaction."

As I spoke, Thom turned to look at me. I wish he hadn't because that's when Smyrna took the opportunity to run. From cell phone to Facebook in a matter of seconds, the picture was blown up and names attached in big black bold lettering. Still running around the internet, for all I know. Of course, it doesn't matter now that the damage is done. When he couldn't stand the accusations of his classmates, Thom dropped out of high school. Works on a farm, somewhere way out. Keeps to himself, I heard. Without Thom, Davin quit teaching adagio. After class on Thursday nights, Lisle and I started going for coffee. Sometimes Davin came along, and we reminisced about old times. We all kept saying that one of these days, we'd head out to the farm, pay Thom a visit. We never did.

Pavlova

Recipe

5 jumbo egg whites, room temperature, if the room is cold and
     dark
1 1/4 cups caster sugar kept dry, despite dampness
scant 2 teaspoons brown malt vinegar
1 1/2 cups cold, fresh whipping cream
1 tablespoon sifted cornflour
4 ripe kiwis
2 ripe passion fruit

1. Wielding a wire whisk, mix whites with vigor, as if your arm and hand have suddenly become possessed by the desire to dance. Stop when whites begin to take on shapes of things you'd rather forget.
2. One tablespoon at a time, add sugar, whisking relentlessly until you can see the shadow of your sweaty face glistening in the meringue.
3. Spoon mixture onto metal tray lined with parchment to avoid stickiness.
4. With rubber spatula, smooth into shape of theater in the round.
5. Bake at medium temperature for 90 minutes or until pavlova is hardened and dry, like a brand-new *pointe* shoe, ready to break in.
6. Having switched off oven, open door and leave ajar for dessert to rest briefly.
7. Whisk cream in chilled bowl until peaks resemble scenery from Kingdom of Snow.
8. Peel and slice fruit into *corps de ballet* of equal portions.
9. Decorate cooled pavlova with cream and fruit.
10. Serve immediately after final standing ovation.
Note: Dessert is delicate yet unwieldy. Be careful with assemblage.

Notes on recipe

Created and named in honor of Russian ballerina Anna Pavlova after her 1926 tour to New Zealand, the dessert is well-known worldwide. This version has no author or date of publication. We don't even know what country it comes from, but the terms *cornflour* and *caster sugar* help to exclude the United States, where Pavlova dreaded dancing in 1913. However, a prominent food anthropologist classifies the references to meringue as distinctly American. Handwritten in elegant script, this recipe appears to exist only on a 3-by-5 note card sandwiched in a collection belonging to American balletmistress Zella Muris of Missouri. The ingredients are basic. No one at Midwest City Ballet, where Muris works, is known to have allergies to any of them. But one thing's for sure: When Alexander Green first ate the pavlova, he morphed into one of the strongest male dancers of all time.

Notes on prima ballerina

Pavlova lived to be one of the world's greatest and most celebrated ballerinas. Still worshipped by many a dancer, the Russian icon of grace is known for her elegance, etiquette, and determination. Despite her allegiance to all things feminine, she presided with a heavy hand over her male partners. If they failed to live up to her expectations, she slapped them, often in public. Eighty-two years after her death, Pavlova is still recognized for her ability to intoxicate audiences, particularly through the roles of the Dying Swan and the Butterfly.

Corrine's perspective

I don't like to say negative shit, but Alex Green is too short to be in the company. Most of the women are at least two inches taller. And at 25, he isn't getting any younger. Why he was hired I'll never know. Politics. To make things worse, he's oh-so-holier than thou: "Ballet is my lover, my life." Give me a break. Probably a latent homosexual. Worst kind. And Zella, his little advocate, she's too old and dried up for anything. Couple of bitches: both of 'em. Well, at least one's gone. You know, before he left, that excuse of a man got away with violating the company contract. Nobody can get that big and buff in such a short time. Must've taken something. Or Zella slipped it to him. Probably a witch.

That's what you should be investigating—the two of them, not me.

Dancer's Contract, Midwest City Ballet, Section 7B

Despite requests for dancers to lose or gain weight, which may be issued at any time (See Section 35C), the Company officially condemns any self-destructive behavior, including but not limited to actions that resemble or lead to the development of eating disorders, to the consumption of illegal substances, and to unwarranted surgical and other medical procedures. Dancers who fail to comply with this edict will be dismissed and replaced immediately.

Excerpt from a review of Midwest City Ballet's winter performance

Grafton's *Lightness of Foot* pays tribute to the devil-may-care playfulness of Gugnoni's score. A series of vignettes that fluctuate between petit allegro and adagio movements combine classical vocabulary with contemporary gestures, making the choreography as light and up-to-date as the dancing. However, an unwelcome serving of irony was offered up in the section titled "Whipped Topping," when one of the dancers landed heavily from a series of jumps.

Tony's take

Corrine is the one who landed like a lead weight in that performance. Of course nobody'll admit it, including Grafton, and he's the artistic director. Corrine didn't just come down heavy; she would've fallen if it hadn't been for Alex. When he saw what was happening, he placed his hands on the small of her back to keep her upright. Instead of thanking her savior, the bitch issued a complaint—said Alex caused her to land funny because he was standing too close. Alex denied it, there was a company hearing, and nothing happened. Grafton stood up for Corrine, and Zella for Alex. Us dancers thought it was all over, but Corrine refused to give up. Had to find something to cause more grief. So she got out the contract. Convinced Grafton that Alex was underweight.

Notes on Zella

If you saw her walking down the street, you'd know, despite the cropped, white hair and slight limp on the left, that Zella Muris was and is a ballerina. Not a modern one, but the kind you read about in books. A woman organized equidistantly between vertebrae—so elegant that even the most inept and poorly mannered step aside to let her pass. Her figure is trim, her expression amenable. Once she was great. Zella's voice feels like maple syrup filling the squares of a waffle. When she speaks, dancers listen. You are one of the few. You have been chosen for a life unlike any other. Sex, family, computers: they come later. You won't relate, no matter how hard you try. Going to the bathroom: even that is different. Doctors will see the X-rays and say something is wrong with your spine. It is straight because you know how to stand straight. You are a dancer. Like the members of the Imperial Ballet—the first, along with political officials to be escorted to safety when invasion was imminent, you are commissioned to preserve order in a world of chaos.

Excerpt I from Alex's diary, left in a storage unit on the outskirts of town

Zella wants to talk. I know what she's going to say—gain weight or my contract is up, except that's not how she'll say it. She'll speak in a way that makes me feel both special and unworthy. Must have been a nun in another life. Huge surprise! Zella's invited me to dinner! Tells me not to worry. Dessert's fantastic. Meringue cream thing with kiwi and passion fruit—named after Pavlova. Don't know why, but feeling lightheaded, kinda giddy. Zella loves the way I jump. Must have forgotten about the contract. Feeling too good to worry.

Interview with Tony

Yes, it's true: Alex gained ten pounds and not a bit of body fat. The whole thing happened in a week, when Zella fed him the pavlova. He said he loved it; it gave him confidence. You have to understand: Alex is straight-laced. That means no drugs, no alcohol, no smokes—nothing. Not even caffeine, and that includes chocolate. No, he's not religious. Married and monogamous to his art. Probably straight. Just my luck. Alex started acting strange after he ate the dessert. Started going out late at night. Said he wanted to get in touch with nature. What that has to do with getting buff I'll never know. With extra activity, he'd be losing weight, not gaining it. But, as you can see in the picture, the man looks like a god—one of those Greek statues you see at museums.

Notes on Alex's picture

No one knows who took it or where it came from, but the pic is running around the internet. Alex's expression is confident yet distant, the open-lipped smile a sign of ease, the far-off gaze an indication that part of him is somewhere else. His outfit is contemporary—light blue form-fitting sleeveless shirt and red skinny jeans, which outline his forceful chest and powerful quads and calves. Yet somehow he appears anachronistic, as if he came from another time, and someone photoshopped the clothes onto his body. His curly hair appears almost as a halo. Around the lower right corner of Alex's lip is a tiny speck of white—not milk, for the consistency appears thick like whipped cream or meringue before it is baked.

Interview with Zella

The recipe is basically sugar, egg whites, cream, and some fruit. Ask anyone with the least bit of knowledge of nutrition, not to mention anatomy and physiology, and you will see that what you propose is preposterous. Of course *I* am no expert, but these are hardly the substances that build muscle. I made the pavlova to cheer up a downtrodden dancer. That's all. Alexander worked very hard to perfect his art. Why not give *him* the credit? Yes, it may appear to some that he developed quickly, but I'm sure you are familiar with the concept of hyperbole. Dancers are notorious for it. Life is either perfect or doomed, performances great or worthless. No, I'm not sure where the recipe originated. It's been in my family for generations. Of course I miss Alexander. He was one of our finest.

Interview with Grafton

I have no idea where Alex went after he left the company. We don't keep tabs on our former dancers. Have you checked the internet? How about the IRS? Now I really must be going. I have a meeting with the Midwest Prairie Alliance. Our company is collaborating with conservationists to preserve classical ballet, the nation's most unappreciated and endangered art form, alongside the prairie, the nation's most unappreciated and endangered ecosystem. If you want to do a story on this exciting development, I'd be happy to meet with you next week.

Alex's Diary, Entry 2

She makes me call her Mademoiselle, and I must bow whenever she enters the room. At first I thought it was a dream, but once she slapped me, I knew Anna Pavlova was real. It's true: she's as light as the dessert created in Her name. Pavlova is teaching me all kinds of things I never really knew. When a man dances with a woman, he must worship her. He must make it look as though he's in charge, but underneath it all, she is. That's how it works. She wakes me up at three in the morning. I bow and kneel before her, and then we head out to the prairie preserve. When I'm with Anna, I never feel cold. The stage is filled with leftover snow and dirt, but somehow we manage. We rehearse until six, and then I take her back to the apartment. We share a slice of pavlova, and then she disappears until the next night. Despite all the extra activity, I feel rested, ready to dance. My body is changing—fast.

Tony's final statement

There's something I forgot to say. Before tech rehearsal for the spring performances, I went to wish Alex *merde*—that's what dancers say instead of good luck or, God forbid, break a you-know-what. Well, I got to his dressing room door and stopped short. I distinctly heard a woman with a Russian accent screaming at him. Then what sounded like a slap. When I knocked at the door, I heard furniture crashing to the floor. When Alex opened the door, the left side of his face was all red, a chair was overturned, and the room was empty, except for the two of us. Yes, I'm sure. I know what I heard and saw.

Excerpt from a review of Midwest City Ballet's spring performance

Rarely do soloists outshine the principals, but such was the case in Grafton's *Prairie Progression*, when Alexander Green and Tony Perugina took flight in a feverish series of man-to-man suspension lifts and supported jumps. Reminiscent of lightning spawning a wildfire, the two men epitomized not only the strength and beauty of the male form but also the stoicism of our ancestors arriving in covered wagons. Kudos to Grafton and his collaboration with the Midwest Prairie Alliance. Good luck to MCB. With dancing and choreography like this, companies on the coasts can't compare.

Alex's diary, last entry

Last night was strange. We talked more than we danced. Both captivated by nature—open landscapes, beetles crawling in grass. Think I'm falling in love. Anna says she could easily replace Corrine. Finally together in front of an audience. I asked how she planned to do it. She made a joke—called herself The Phantom of the Ballet. I laughed. Asked why she didn't go to New York. "Because you are here," she said. I'll never forget those words. My wrists slipped during a press lift, and she punched me. The frozen grass clinked in the wind. The prairie was laughing.

Notes on YouTube video

Extensive investigation, but no one knows who posted the video or where it came from. It's called *Boa*. The picture is clear: Alexander Green partnering none other than Anna Pavlova. Alex looks like a Greek myth come to life—beige dance belt and nothing else but his sparkling brown ringlets dripping with sweat as he lifts his partner high in the air. Pavlova, skin tanned and expression distant, sports a black bikini. Her hair is buzzed to a bristle. The choreography is twenty-first century— unabashedly sexual, moments of sustained extension followed by repetitive, spastic moves: peace and then the storm. Pavlova constricts her partner to death. The final scene focuses on Alex, eyes rolled back, face blue, expression slack. Three comments posted on the accompanying YouTube page: "bout time," from sexyladycub; "gr8 hairdo pavvy," from pickleloverspoon; "What happened to human tenderness? Violence gratuitous," from MidwestSpiritWeaver.

Excerpt from Arts section of *Midwest Tribune*

Despite local, state, and national funding, Midwest City Ballet and the Midwest Prairie Alliance received a heavy blow today. Late Summer Dance on the Prairie, held at and supported by the privately owned Midwest Prairie Preserve for the last 40 years, will be discontinued. The land has been sold to the Mall-Mart Corporation, and construction for a new Mall-Mart Megacomplex will begin within the month. The site will include multiple stores, a ballpark, two daycare centers, a one-acre prairie preserve, and a new four-year college featuring the highly popular Corporate Studies major. "Once the construction is done, the ballet can perform at the ballpark," said Hugo Spitz, spokesman for the multimillion-dollar project. Midwest City Ballet Artistic Director Frederick Grafton, who received the International Green Space Choreographic Award earlier this year, was unavailable for comment.

Front-page story in *Midwest Tribune*

Mall-Mart Project Swallowed Up

After a month of rumors and jokes claiming the Mall-Mart Megacomplex was jinxed, haunted, and doomed, the project caved in on itself—literally. Only two days after the completion of nine buildings and a ballpark, a giant sinkhole swallowed up everything except one acre of prairie, leaving no trace of the 80 million dollar complex. No one was injured, since the cave-in happened sometime between 3 and 6 a.m., according to police. A worker who wishes to remain anonymous said he found piles of kiwi peel at the construction site during the last month. The cause of the sinkhole is under investigation.

Statement from a baker in rural North Dakota

Fat little dude—called himself Al Green. Hired him because of the look on his face. Real depressed. Getting out of a bad relationship, he said. Only worked here a short time. Crazy about the prairie, he was. Talented baker. Never tasted a pavlova like the ones he made. So light—gave you energy, made you want to dance.

The Belly Dance

When an experienced belly dancer performs an abdominal undulation, the body appears to fluctuate between solid and liquid forms, between reality and a dream state. Through mesmerizing circular movements, the belly dancer brings us back to the womb, titillates our libido, makes us hungry for sensation. It is no coincidence that belly dancing is often coupled with eating. Middle Eastern restaurants make the most money on belly-dance nights, when watching dance and eating merge into a single sensory experience. Since the turn of the twenty-first century, belly dancing has become extremely popular among American women of European descent, particularly those who are pregnant. Frustrated with her husband's inability to give her a child, Karla, a 36-year-old librarian and hardcore foodie, begins to explore multiple forms of belly dancing.

The door sticks as Karla tries the knob—just enough noise to whip Pippa into a frenzy, her fat black tail slapping the floor as she scratches from the inside.

"You're just going to have to wait," says Karla, tired of the door, the dog, the house.

Turning out her feet like a ballet dancer, Karla widens her stance to get a better grip on the knob. The dog starts to bark.

"Pippa, no!"

The dog lets out a whimper and scratches harder. Not until the third try does Karla gain entry, her stomach rattled by the tumult of turning and pushing. As she makes her way to the kitchen, the scent of stale urine embedded in the worn-out shag enters her nose. Her stomach feels as if it's dancing the polka, food and enzymes popping around in 3/4 time. Karla fills Pippa's water bowl, and the dog slathers her long runner's legs with thick, foamy saliva.

"Get away from me, you stupid old dog," cries Karla. "When will you ever learn? I'm not Jennifer."

Turner had divorced Jennifer three years before he met Karla. He ended up with the dog and the house, while Jennifer got the kids, the cabin, and enough alimony and child support to sell the cabin and buy a new house.

"Good thing for you we're not in the Philippines," says Karla, as the dog wags its tail. "Stewed with vinegar and peppercorns: that's what you'd be. 'Wedding style,' they call it. A delicacy."

Karla and Turner had first met in the produce section of the Stop and Shop. He was holding a jicama in one hand while fingering it with the other. About six feet tall, slightly heavy around the waist, and dressed in a sweatshirt and jeans, he looked out of place—the sort she'd expect in the beer aisle hefting a couple twelve-packs, not the produce section examining a root vegetable as though it were breathing in his hand.

"Keep that up, and you might get arrested," said Karla, shocked by the forwardness of her statement.

Turner dropped the vegetable, and they both stood there as it rolled between their carts.

"Now look what you made me do," said Turner, laughing as he reached down to pick up the jicama.

Feeling a slight chill, Karla remembered she was wearing a pair of running shorts and a tank top. She turned away and rushed to the opposite end of the store. The two met again in the ethnic aisle. She was looking for coconut manna, and he, Thai red curry sauce. By the time they reached the checkout, they had made a dinner date. When Turner called to cancel— he had to operate on a cat's kidney—Karla returned to the store, purchased a jicama, and went home to make a salad. She ended up leaving it with Turner's receptionist. A Great Dane escaped its owner and ate it. But Turner was more than touched by the gesture and offered to cook dinner the following night—beef brisket hash with pickled beets. Karla was hooked. Despite the age difference—he was 46 and she 33—they had similar likes and dislikes, and the sexual energy was more than adequate. They savored good food and worked together amicably in the kitchen. Turner was the first person she had met, who, just like she, used Q-tips to clean the garlic press. Karla and Turner soon found out they had the same outlook on life: time off was meant to be spent traveling. Neither Jennifer nor Karla's ex-boyfriends wanted to go anywhere. After six months of dating, Karla and

Turner got married.

Surrounded by low-slung pines, the house blends in with its exurban counterparts—colonial-style saltbox with cheap metal shutters that no one uses. The corrugated shingles give away the structure as a child of the sixties. Unlike the living room, the kitchen is modernized. Turner had hired a contractor to do the job as a wedding present to Karla. They postponed the honeymoon to Paris, when the improvements cost more than expected. In three years, when Turner's son Peter reaches 18 and no longer requires child support, they might have enough to travel. These days they barely get out of Rhode Island.

After taking the dog for a quick run, Karla chews an antacid. Then she slices her Ginsu into a fresh pumpkin. Two hours later, Turner enters the kitchen, holding his left arm behind his back. Pippa comes running. When the dog licks his arm, he looks at Karla, a crooked smile creeping onto his face.

"Get away from him," snaps Karla, dropping her ladle into the pot of Thai pumpkin soup. She turns to her husband. "OK, show me the arm. Let's see the damage."

"It's not bad," says Turner, revealing a fresh set of scratches: solid stripes oozing orange-red from elbow to wrist.

"Don't tell me—your old friend Percival. Or was it Medea, or, better yet, Furkin?"

"Percy didn't mean it. I had to give him a shot."

Karla imagines her husband dying of rabies—unable to speak, foaming at the mouth. "You know you could've patched up the wounds before driving home."

"I didn't want to be late and make you nervous," he says. "You know how you sometimes get."

Karla lets out a sigh.

Known for accepting pets from Providence to New London, Turner never refuses a sick animal, even when the owner is short on cash. Turner's kindness is both irresistible and unnerving. Once, in the middle of making love, he heard an animal screech. Not until he had removed the porcupine quills from the back end of the neighbor's goat did Turner and Karla get back to what they were doing. At least he wasn't cheating on her with another woman, or, like her last boyfriend, with another man.

"If you charge extra for every scratch and cut," says Karla, "we could both retire and move to Newport."

"Sure could," says Turner, blowing on his arm. "Spend our summers on the water."

Karla has dreamed of sailing from New England to Florida, stopping at gyms and gourmet restaurants along the way. Then she would write a bestselling travel guide—something that combines adventure, food, and exercise. As a librarian, she knows books. Without children to tie her down, she could put her skills and creativity to better use by writing one. All she needs is some training, along with the time and money to travel and write.

"Sounds like a plan," says Karla. "And we can save the sea turtles, while we're at it."

Turner has dreamed of joining a group of volunteers to carry loggerheads from their nests to the Atlantic. He had arranged to do just that in Georgia, but ended up marrying Karla, instead.

Turner and Karla know that neither dream will transpire, not after three years of marriage, not in the midst of an economic downturn, when they're lucky to have jobs and a roof over their heads. Yet neither one will give up the possibility of adventure, excitement. They think about it, talk about it. Once, while they were enjoying ostrich steaks with a newlywed couple at a restaurant in Westerly, they had a similar discussion—same story, a few embellishments. In private, the wife asked Karla if she and Turner were making plans or exchanging "subtle jabs."

Karla said, "A little of both, kind of like a dance."

Despite the disappointments, Turner and Karla have each other, which is more than she can say about her relationship with her mother and sister. Neither one visits, not since Pippa pooped and peed on their belongings last Christmas.

"Your place is a mess," said her mother, a retired ballet director visiting from South Carolina. "Get rid of that damned dog, fix up the house, and I might make the trip in the summer."

Karla's mother has never liked Turner. She considers him boring and low class—too mild-mannered and "earthy" to be a "real man." Born Eunice Schtookenbach in Bayonne, New Jersey, her mother changed her name when she got a better job in a better ballet company. To both fans and foes, she's known as Cynthiana Du Bois. All through Karla's childhood—she never knew her father—Cynthiana put career over family. When it came to cooking, she either boiled chickens or heated up frozen diet TV dinners. At restaurants, the family only ate salads. "Aspiring ballerinas have to watch their weight," the mother said, whenever her daughters begged for something different. Karla kept thin but never made it past Ballet III. At 63, Cynthiana is still svelte and loves to show off her calves.

Turner doesn't care what Cynthiana thinks of him. He loves to wear baggy, unrevealing clothes, and on weekends, he puts together jigsaw puzzles. Lately, since the vet business has fallen into a slump, he bakes bread—lots of it—the old-fashioned way. He says the kneading and punching help him relax. In the past few months, Turner has gained a lot of weight. Of course Karla can't help him eat bread—not the kind he makes. She's gluten intolerant.

* * *

It's Saturday, and Turner and Karla sleep late. As usual, they decide to lounge in bed before breakfast. Karla does her "food exercises," while Turner reads the paper. Thinking of a fruit or vegetable, she contorts her body to match its shape. She came up with the idea when she was 6, when her mother refused to buy an *ube,* or purple yam, on tour in Manila. If Karla couldn't have the vegetable, she'd become it. Karla has always been good at coping creatively.

Without pretext, Turner puts down the paper and suggests she take up a hobby.

"Like what?" says Karla, irritated by the interruption.

"I don't know," says Turner. "But knowing you, you'll think of something."

Karla relaxes her legs and folds her arms. "Well, you must have had a reason for coming up with the suggestion, not to mention a few ideas about what I could do. So tell me."

Turner raises and lowers his shoulders, the same way Peter does, when father asks son how things are going at home. Karla glares at him until he speaks.

"How about hot-air ballooning over the Serengeti?"

"Very funny."

"Well, now that you brought it up, we could use a little humor around here."

Turner is right. Karla's gone bitter. Ever since her mother and sister's Christmas visit, she hasn't been herself. But then again, she knows better than to let down her guard, or she'll end up just like her mother—selfish, mean, and cantankerous, mad about getting old and stiff, unable to perform a simple *plié*, without pain and discomfort. At 36, Karla is aging, perhaps a little slower, thanks to the gym, but not as ungracefully as an old ballerina who can't accept the fact that her time has long passed.

No matter how upset she gets, Karla will never tell Turner to replace the dirty, smelly carpet, which will eventually wear out. Nor will she suggest that he get rid of the 9-year-old incontinent dog—bound to die sooner or later. Furthermore, she'll never let on that she's no longer aroused by her husband's body, which seems to get bigger and yeastier with every loaf he bakes. Karla wishes he would join her at the gym—two-hour workouts, five days a week.

"I do need to do something," says Karla, pointing her feet in fifth position to look like a carrot.

Turner reaches for the newspaper. "Local theater's looking for actors for the upcoming production of *Kismet.*"

"Discipline myself to learn and perfect lines and songs? Not for a bunch of amateurs."

Turner rolls over and kisses his wife, his stomach pressing into her ribs. "'*Strangers in Paradise. All lost in a wonderland.*' You know you'd look fantastic in one of those Middle Eastern belly dance outfits."

Karla lets her feet fall heavily onto the mattress. "Sure you're not confusing me with my sister?"

"No, and there's no need to say such a thing."

"Sorry."

The moment Karla's sister Wendy had arrived last Christmas, she began to flirt with Turner. A former Broadway dancer, Wendy had the body to prove it—"tits and ass" and a perfect little smirk. Politely dismissing the dalliance, Turner told Karla he would stay at the office, if her sister kept it up. Karla confronted Wendy, who responded with a joke about vets and bestiality. Then, when Pippa urinated and defecated in both guest bedrooms, Cynthiana and Wendy left in a huff.

When Turner's first marriage failed, he had a vasectomy. Before he proposed to Karla, he made it clear he would never get a reversal. Since they were married, she has only asked him once. He responded by saying her hips were perfect the way they were. She pressed him some more, and he left the house. Karla followed him to the Portuguese bakery café, where he consumed half a dozen cornflour and raisin cupcakes. She made sure he didn't see her. When he got up to leave, she hurried off to the gym.

* * *

Karla enters the studio, dancers in full force. Looking for a place at the back, she nearly gasps at the roomful of burgeoning bellies, glistening with sweat. She glances at the schedule and realizes she's invaded a class for expectant mothers. Rolling to a syncopated beat, the students' stomachs seem alive but detached. The teacher, a curvy bleached blonde in a black halter-top with dangling silver spangles, shows off her cleavage, as she adjusts the hips and backs of the belly dancers. Karla holds in a laugh, as she imagines her mother reacting to the sight. The teacher wears a plastic nametag above her left breast: Kundini—obviously not her real name.

"I want you to imagine that your belly is a snake, charmed by the music," says Kundini, her voice strong and raspy. "Bend your knees slightly; now feel the impulse."

Kundini changes the music to percussion and flute—a tune that brings back memories of a Persian dive in the old part of Providence, the place where Karla and Turner had polished off bowl after bowl of pomegranate walnut stew on a frigid January night. Karla places her bag in the corner and watches while the teacher roams the room, her stomach undulating "forward, up, down, and back. Forward, up, down, and back." About half

31

have it right, their bellies doing one thing, and the rest of their bodies another. The moves are much harder than they look. As Karla attempts her first undulation, she feels as if her abdomen has turned to stone—too tight and toned to roll and fold, more like a buoy bobbing up and down than a wave rolling toward shore. When she begins to feel nauseated, she sits down. A few minutes later, a middle-aged woman with a melon stomach sits next to her.

"A newbie," says the woman.

Karla nods. In a ballet studio, no one but the teacher speaks during class.

The woman turns to Karla. "Dearie, you don't look so good. Come with me."

The woman helps her to the bathroom, where they both spend the next five minutes throwing up. Despite the stinging in her eyes, Karla feels cleansed—as if she has rid herself of a blockage. She decides to go back to class, but the woman motions for her to sit down on an old couch.

"You don't even look pregnant," says the woman, introducing herself as Janie.

"Thanks," says Karla, not quite ready to correct Janie's mistake. "Still working out Monday through Friday."

"That's great. I can barely get here once a week."

"Long drive?" says Karla, realizing too late that Janie was referring to her pregnancy, not her commute.

"You're funny," says Janie. "Drive's nothing. Live in Mystic."

"Oh, I haven't been there in ages," says Karla. As a teen, she had toured the Mystic aquarium and seen a sperm whale, the Connecticut state animal.

"How far along?" asks Karla, looking at the woman's exposed belly.

"Don't ask," says Janie. "Too far. And if I knew how miserable this pregnancy was going to be, well, let's just leave it at that."

Before Karla can respond, Janie asks about *her* pregnancy. Karla takes a breath and finds herself making up a story about an anonymous donor with German genes and an IQ of 160. "My husband had a vasectomy after his first wife divorced him and sued for child support."

Janie tells her the only good thing about her pregnancy is not listening to her mother-in-law ask when she's going to have a baby. "Test turns out positive, and the next thing I know, I'm initiated into the cult of pregnancy. All of a sudden, everybody's touching my stomach, congratulating me, asking if it's a boy or girl."

Karla feels the rumbling in her own abdomen, wishing that the pain would turn into a fetus.

"I'll tell you," says Janie. "When the baby kicks, I feel like I'm going to land on the opposite end of the room. Nobody ever said it was going to hurt *this* much. On top of that, I'm sick just about every day."

* * *

When Karla gets home, she finds a note on the living room table: "Pippa in trouble. Taking her in. May not make it through the night." When Karla reaches for her coat, she gets dizzy and throws up on the carpet. Cleaning the vomit makes her even weaker, but she can't stand the thought of leaving a mess. She calls Turner.

"How's Pippa?" she asks, suddenly guilty about hating the dog.

"Not good," says Turner. "Doing everything I can."

She tells him she accidentally ate some of his bread and won't be able to join him at the clinic. He asks if she's all right, and she tells him not to worry. He tells her not to wait up, and they hang up the phone.

Karla brushes her teeth and runs the bath. As she's waiting for the water to cool, she does a database search for belly dancing and pregnancy. She finds out that expectant mothers take up the activity "to balance their old and new identities," to let people know they can still "look sexy." Karla places an empty plastic dishpan next to the tub, in case her stomach thinks faster than her legs. The water is so hot she can barely submerge her body. She lets in some cold. Lying on her back, she begins to feel calm. She thinks about the carpet and sits up to wash. Once again on her back, she tries an undulation.

"Forward, up, down, and back," she says aloud. "I wonder if it makes fetuses do somersaults?"

When the movement causes her stomach to churn, she uses her right foot to lift the shower lever, and her left to turn the water to a trickle. Hot, heavy drops land just below her belly button, rolling either forward or back, depending on whether she's breathing out or in. When she holds her breath, the drops fill the depth of her navel and spill over in all directions. Kundini wore a ruby-colored jewel in her belly button. Karla wonders if Turner loves his dog more than her. She turns off the water and allows herself to settle. The vomiting has made her thirsty, but she's afraid to drink. Maybe she's allergic to pregnant women. The shower drips. For a moment the drops come all at once, and then once every half second. She closes her eyes.

Karla dreams she gives birth to a puppy.

When she awakens, a message is waiting on the machine: Pippa is dead. Karla stands before the mirror and attempts to perform an undulation. Her belly is still too stiff. She decides to make dinner—veal cutlet with *Pfifferlinge* mushrooms in cream sauce, followed by a side of white asparagus soup—recipes from her grandmother. When Turner gets home a little after midnight, Karla embraces him tightly.

"I don't know what to say," she says, feeling tension—quite uncharacteristic—in Turner's abdomen. "Pippa will be missed."

"Sit down, Karla."

"Don't you want dinner?"

Turner repeats the command, and Karla turns off the stove and sits at the kitchen table.

"I've had more physical contact with Pippa than you in the last four months," says Turner, his voice somber and quiet. "Just before she died, she licked my hand. You, on the other hand, turn away from me, every chance you get. At this rate, I'm surprised we're still sleeping in the same bed."

Karla opens her mouth to speak, but Turner holds up his hand.

"Yes, I'm fat and undesirable. And yes, I'm to blame for being this way, but not completely. Have you ever looked at the calorie content of the meals you prepare? Don't answer; I'm sure you

34

have, for yourself, for someone who exercises 300-plus days a year, as if she's training for the Olympics."

Tears streaming down her face, Karla slumps in her chair, pain once again rushing to her stomach.

"And yes," says Turner, "I appreciate the trouble you go to, to plan and prepare those meals. In fact, I appreciate them to a fault. The food is fantastic. You put body, mind, and soul into the entire process, but cooking and eating are not the same thing as loving."

As Turner talks, Karla slumps lower, her stomach curling in on itself, sharp pellets of pain pummeling her belly.

"You rope yourself off from the rest of the world," he says, "with your perfect meals, your perfect workouts—so Germanic, so balletic."

Karla unfolds herself and stands.

"You started it," she says, her voice barely a whisper. "You're the one who roped himself off, literally, with a vasectomy. Nothing in this house, with the exception of the kitchen, is mine." Karla's voice gets louder. "It's all Jennifer—Jennifer's furniture, Jennifer's children's old toys, Jennifer's dog. How do you think it makes me feel, knowing that no matter how much passion I exert, we will always be roped off from each other, roped off in a setting that reminds me you used to be different, different with someone else?"

Turner places his hands on his wife's shoulders. They stand facing each other in silence. Each is breathing heavily.

"Why didn't you tell me?" says Turner.

"I tried to once," says Karla. "You wouldn't let me."

Turner lets go, and Karla takes a deep breath. They look at each other in silence. Without thinking or shifting her gaze, Karla feels her belly beginning to undulate. Her shoulders, elbows, and wrists assume the posture of twin cobras, straddled by her head and torso, performing in unison. Without a word, Karla leads Turner into the bedroom. When he enters his wife, deep in the early hours of the morning, she accidentally bites his arm, her tongue brushing the scab drawn by the claws of Percival. Turner reacts with a shiver, and Karla attempts to apologize, but the taste of her husband's arm keeps her from moving, stops her from speaking. Beyond the salt of his sweat and grit of his blood is a gustative sensation altogether new and utterly delicious. Karla has broken through. By sampling Turner's arm, she has ingested the man she loves—the skilled surgeon, the animal lover, her lover. Karla rolls her tongue. Turner dances through her mouth—forward, up, down, and back. Karla swallows. Her stomach no longer hurts.

The Dancing Plague

Strasbourg, France: Summer 1518

Her legs kicking, arms flailing, and hips twitching, Frau Troffea moves through the crowded, narrow streets. She says nothing, her expression distant, her mouth vibrating. As the movements intensify, rivulets of sweat stream down the furrows of her face. Troffea's onlookers, including nuns and priests, beggars and traders, stand back as they grow fearful of her relentless spasms, shivers, and jolts. The dance, if one could call it that, lasts several days, with minimal breaks, no music, and a considerable amount of blood flowing from the woman's tired and swollen feet. Troffea's dance is only the beginning. By early August, an epidemic has formed—a hundred or so citizens have succumbed to the Dancing Plague. The mysterious affliction lasts until late August or early September.

Midway Atoll: Autumn 1987

On a flat, grassy patch, separating beach from forest, a birdwatcher studies a pair of dancing Laysan albatrosses. Extending their yellow bills, they emit a *moo* sound, before engaging in a series of breast ripples, accompanied by whistles and snaps. Taking a picture at just the right moment, the birdwatcher captures both male and female bodies forming the shape of a heart, as their bills intertwine in a step called the bill touch. The birdwatcher knows better than to mistake the dance as a mating ritual; after all, pairs dance for around two years before copulation occurs. The recurring dance serves as a process of recognition, in which a pair bond is formed. To assure that the bond will last, the birds get to know each other's personalities and idiosyncrasies through the performance of dance. The birdwatcher is divorced; her husband had lied about liking birds.

Red Lodge, Montana: Summer 1987

Fifteen-year-old Travis Coot tells his mother he was switched at birth, that he belongs to wealthy New Yorkers touring the West when their son was born—patrons of the arts, who would send him to private school and dance lessons. Travis fits the mold of a Montana cowboy as John Wayne embodies the persona of ballet dancer. The boy's buttocks are overdeveloped, and his upper body is too small to ride a horse and rope cattle. He hates the open range and has no interest in anything having to do with the West. Ever since he can remember, he has danced—in the bathroom, the back of the horse barn, anywhere. His moves, repetitive and bombastic, often make the horses kick, but that doesn't stop Travis, who thinks the animals are just trying to dance. "My name is Nijinsky Vanderbilt," he says. "The real Travis Coot is living a life of misery and punishment in New York. He's a Montana cowboy. All we need to do is find each other and make the switch." Travis's parents call him loony, his classmates beat him up, and his grandmother tells him to start planning, if he ever wants to get out of Hell.

The Vosges: Summer 1518

When her dancing becomes too much for the citizens of Strasbourg, Frau Troffea is transported to the foothills of the Vosges. Far too exhausted to protest, the woman lies prostrate, as she is carried thirty miles through forests, fields, and orchards to a dank grotto and chapel dedicated to St. Vitus. Once tempted by dancing women to relinquish his Christianity and pledge allegiance to Diocletian and the Roman gods, the burgeoning saint refrained. After a few hundred years of Christian prayer and worship, Vitus became known for exerting a bit of vengeance. If people got out of hand, he supposedly made them dance— excessively—until they died. According to physician-alchemist Paracelsus, the frau danced to humiliate her husband, after he had asked her to do something she didn't want to do, thus causing the saint to wreak his vengeance. However, there is no record of what the frau said or thought.

Midway Atoll: Autumn 1987

Female Laysan albatrosses—the birdwatcher knows this— look for a lessening of male aggression during the pairing process. This fact is quite evident in the Midway pair, as the male responds to the female during the dance. The male moves his head sideways, just prior to tucking it in his feathers, relinquishing his power in order to honor his potential life mate. The movements are referred to as scapular action. These and other dance moves reflect a distinct reduction of aggression, which helps to assure the female that her potential nesting site will be a place of peace and tranquility. Also, females judge the worth of males by their ability to dance. When the birdwatcher began to date the man she recently divorced, they went dancing. A commercial pilot with no dance experience, he stepped on her feet three times, apologizing emphatically after each injury. She forgave him. After he told her about the time he tipped the plane to avoid a flock of geese, they got married. He moved into her house. When he wanted a TV in the room overlooking her bird feeders, they got one. After a year of blaring weather reports, accompanied by shouts, grunts, burps, and guffaws, the rare and elusive indigo bunting stopped frequenting the feeders. The birdwatcher divorced her husband; she knows that Laysan albatrosses bond for life.

Red Lodge: Autumn 1987

A tractor-trailer operator, Travis Coot's father lives for competitive sports. He relishes football almost as much as he does the truck he drives and the hats he wears. Luckily he has a son named Russ, whom he counts on "to act normal." Russ has won blue ribbons for roping cattle and just made it onto the high school football team. Russ more than makes up for Travis, whom his father tries to ignore. Now 16, Travis works as a janitor in a local dance studio. It doesn't take long before the teacher agrees to give him free lessons in ballet, tap, and jazz. Travis knows the teacher lacks experience and talent, but the classes make him feel human. For every dollar he earns, his grandmother adds two. The deal is their "little secret," she says. "At least one member of this family will aspire to something more than a truck driver or cowpoke." Travis's grandmother grew up in a city. She really knows how to dance. On Sundays, when Travis spends the afternoon at her house, she teaches him the fox trot, waltz, tango, and rumba.

Strasbourg: Autumn 1518

Divine intervention is credited for the loss of hundreds of citizens of Strasbourg, who follow in Frau Troffea's footsteps. According to one account, God and the saints are enraged by widespread corruption. Leading lives of luxury and hedonism, clerics copulate with nuns, who slay their newborns and bury the bodies beneath churches. Confessions given by mortal sinners are null and void, damnation imminent. Another hypothesis comes from physicians, who identify the dancing disease as a symptom of overheated blood. Borrowing from humoral theory put forth by Hippocrates in the 300s, sixteenth-century doctors prescribe more dancing. "Sweat it out," they say, preparing the way for elaborate functions, in which hired musicians and companion dancers are provided to help cure the Dancing Plague. In a grand affair, Troffea's friends, neighbors, and relatives dance before the horse market, their feet tapping, arms flapping, and bodies running around like fowl whose heads have succumbed to the ax. It doesn't take long for more people to die dancing.

Midway Atoll: Autumn 1987

The birdwatcher sketches a likeness of dancing Laysan albatrosses tucking their heads underneath their wings. Standing up, she attempts to imitate the dance and scares away the birds. She realizes her armpits are beginning to smell, smiling at the thought of how unappealing she would appear, if an eligible bachelor were to walk by: legs unshaved, hair dripping with sweat, glasses steamy and smudged. On her way back to the hotel room, she spots a masked booby on the beach, its nest a few feet away in a shallow depression. She remembers her first sighting. On their honeymoon in Hawaii, she and her husband were walking along the coast when she spotted the elusive yellow-eyed bird with brown-and-white markings. Instead of rejoicing in her find, her husband grabbed her right breast and squeezed it. The feeling reminded her of a mammogram. Masked boobies generally lay two eggs, one for keeps and the other for insurance.

If both hatch, one sibling kills the other.

Red Lodge and New York: Summer 1988

Russ says his brother Travis is hopeless. "Keep dancing and everyone'll think you're a faggot." Travis says they already do and he doesn't care. Russ is dating Chrissie, a born-again Christian who claims that dancing is bad. "Keep it up, and you'll end up dead," says Chrissie, whenever she sees her boyfriend's brother. Travis has saved a thousand dollars for his new life in New York. "You'll need a lot more than that," says his grandmother, who's set up an audition at a private arts school in Manhattan. The flight gets bumpy when they pass over the Mississippi. Travis can no longer see land but refuses to get scared. His grandmother takes a pill. At the audition, someone flips on the music—new wave, jazz, and classical, one form merging into the next. As Travis kicks and bounces and leaps, he knows he'll never move back home. The teachers welcome him with a full scholarship and stipend. The director calls him "rough but talented, a Montana sapphire trapped beneath layers of ugly rock." Travis says goodbye to his grandmother. They both cry.

Cyberspace: Now and Then

According to a celebrated scholar, the citizens of Strasbourg entered a deep, trance-like state when they succumbed to uncontrollable bouts of dance. A result of the stresses of famine and hardship, the dancing trance failed to lift people out of their misery, for all they could do was conjure up visions of demons, angry saints, and other sinister entities. In the midst of trying to escape their fears, they did the opposite and died.

New York: Autumn 1988

The City isn't exactly what Travis had expected, but he's grateful for the opportunity to dance. When he's not dancing, he studies English, math, history, and science. A girl with curly bangs similar to Chrissie's says, "AIDS is a gay disease, but as long as you don't have sex or take drugs, you don't get it." Travis feels homesick and takes a walk through Central Park, the place his grandmother has told him not to go. At the edge of a dirt trail, he sees for the first time a male couple having sex. He is both disgusted and aroused. Not sure what to do, he takes off, but when he rounds the next corner, he nearly runs into the birdwatcher. "Watch where you're going," she says, irritated that Travis may have scared away the one warbler she has yet to mark on her life list. "Sorry," says Travis, his heart pummeling his chest. As he walks off, the birdwatcher notices the gracefulness of his gait.

Saverne: Spring 2013

No one knows how long Frau Troffea lived after she was offered up at the shrine of St. Vitus.

New York: Spring 1989

Travis picks up a pamphlet about AIDS and learns there is no cure. There is a boy in his ballet class he likes. He's not sure if the boy likes him back, but when they accidentally brush arms in front of the water fountain, he feels a shiver of energy. When Travis sees the boy looking at him, he feigns a sneeze, tucking his head in his armpit like a Laysan albatross, a bird he read about in his science book. In history, Travis is learning about medieval Europe. When the teacher asks him what he knows about the subject, he says that people back then were religious and poor, dirty and superstitious. Sometimes, when he wakes up and can't fall back to sleep, Travis dances late into the night.

The Nebraska Hula

Ingrid's Special Notes on Hula Video

Only when something moves her greatly does Ingrid write notes in her pocket notebook—hardback black cover with a red velvet ribbon used to mark pages, given to her last year by her husband, just before he died, for her 70th birthday.

Hawaiian hula dancers remind me of Nebraska corn swaying in the rain. The tide encroaches, drenching waves washing over grass skirts—legs, torsos, and arms moving in unison. I wonder how they'd look if they moved the dance from the Pacific to the prairie. So sensual yet spiritual as they chant, *E Pele e Pele,* in honor of the volcano goddess. The Nebraska Panhandle has a few ancient remnants of lava cones. The hula dance tells the story of Volcano Goddess Pele, who meets a warrior named Ohia and asks him to marry her. When Ohia claims his love for Lehua, Pele transforms him into a twisted tree. Expressing compassion for Lehua, the gods turn her into a flower that blossoms on the twisted tree. A legend says the lovers will be together for eternity, unless Pele decides to spew lava and kill the tree. Some say ohia trees rustling in the wind gave birth to the hula. While enjoying an island vacation in 1872, Mark Twain claimed that hula dancers moved in "perfect concert," as "hands, arms, bodies, limbs, and heads waved, swayed, gesticulated, bowed, stooped, whirled, squirmed, twisted and undulated as if they were part and parcel of a single individual." Christian missionaries and sugar planters nearly wiped out the sacred dance. When the hula made its way to California, many denounced it as sordid, sacrilegious cavorting. Sounds just like Nicole in a fundamentalist fit.

A Conversation between Ingrid's Son Michael and his Wife Nicole

The two sit in wicker chairs on their tiny Southern California patio, featuring a view of a seven-foot, stained wooden fence flanking their neighbor's beige stucco ranch. In the background they can hear birds chirping, and, on the other side of the fence, their neighbor clinking ice in a glass while ordering pizza.

Michael: We need to go see my mother.

Nicole: In January in Nebraska?

Michael: How about early spring?

Nicole: Even worse. Either we get a snowstorm or a tornado. Can't you convince her to move somewhere closer, so we can visit her whenever we like? I mean I love her dearly, but . . .

Michael: No, you don't, so please don't say that you do. But I appreciate your relying on your faith in Jesus to treat her the best you can.

Nicole: You know I do care about her, even if it's more for your sake. I pray for Ingrid's forgiveness every single day and night.

Michael: Sometimes you remind me of my mother—always trying to be the boss. My mother's an agnostic hippie librarian. Her interests are too scattered. She'll never convert.

Nicole: Sometimes I wonder about *your* faith.

Michael: Don't.

Nicole: But if she moved into Orangeland or Almond Tree Retirement, she'd be around people her own age, and with the two of us nearby, we might even get her to church.

Michael: Never.

Nicole: A few scattered houses and a bunch of farmland: that's the extent of her neighborhood. And who are her friends now that your father is gone? A middle-aged homosexual who inherited a farmhouse? What if something happens to her?

Michael: Her friend's name is Mario.

Ingrid's Recipe for Hawaiian Coconut Salad for Docu-Night at Mario's

Although the septuagenarian watches both her sugar and salt intake, Ingrid likes to indulge in what she calls 'trashy sweets' every now and then.

1 can Florida's Best mandarin oranges
1 can Dole crushed pineapple

½ bag Baker's sweetened coconut
1 jar Michigander maraschino cherries
1 cup Land O Snow sour cream
1 cup Dannon plain yogurt
1 bag Fuffer-Fluffer miniature marshmallows

Directions: Fast from eating sugar for at least a week and then mix all ingredients and refrigerate to set. Serve sparingly.

An Excerpt from Ingrid's Diary

Unlike her pocket notebook, Ingrid's diary appears in wire-bound notebooks bought at the local dollar store. Depending on her mood and/or what's on sale, she writes in a variety of colors—always in pen. The following section is written in pink.

The other day I was going through an old trunk in the attic—still trying to downsize before I get too old—and guess what I found? One of those plastic Hawaiian hula dolls people used to mount on the dashboard. Michael used to collect them. Must have had it on the Olds Delta 88. Drive that old boat on Nebraska gravel, and aloha Hawaii. I can just see that little hula dancer swiveling those hips a mile a minute, as tires on stone rap out a drum medley that'd make you sit back, close your eyes, and order a Mai Tai. Tackiest thing I ever saw: that fat little doll. Cabbage green grass skirt made of God knows what, faded pink lei that reminds me of a foot fungus I had as a little girl, and a jaundiced flower-print halter top not unlike Charlotte Perkins Gilman's description of sinister wallpaper.

The doll kind of reminds me of Nicole. Had a good mind to wrap it up and send it to California. Then I thought twice. I'm sure Nicole would find a way to use it against me—tell Michael I finally lost my mind. Speaking of losing it, I nearly did, according to one smart-mouthed store clerk. Arthritis started acting up when I was chopping onions for French onion soup earlier in the week. So, I got in the car and went all the way to Lincoln to buy a mandolin. A real doozy of a clerk named Pumice or

Peyton or some idiotic nonsense like that—she thought I was loopy, all because she was too dumb to know that a mandolin is a kitchen tool used for slicing vegetables. So much for working in the kitchen department at Muncie's. All I can say is let her try to chop onions with twisted fingers like mine. Probably doesn't even know how to cook. No one does these days. No one except chefs and the old people. The rest just order pizza and eat out. Puma or Putrid—whatever her name was—eventually found the mandolin, but never in my life did I feel so insulted when all I did was ask a question. She looked at me as if I had lost my marbles. Nicole is just like that, which is partly why I don't want to go to California. My life is here, even without Hank.

Shaken, Not Stirred

This is Ingrid's favorite radio show, which she listens to faithfully every Friday night. Over the phone, Michael taught her how to download the show, which she now puts on CDs to listen to in the car. That's the closest mother and son manage to get these days, when Michael teaches her how to do something on the computer.

You're listening to Shaken, Not Stirred, the home of lounge, mod-squad pop, and exotica from the land of martinis, Mai Tais, and fallout shelters. I'm Darren Brigadoon, coming to you from Midwestern State University here at 91.3 on your listening dial. Brrr: it's cold out there. I don't know about you, but I've had enough winter. For the next two hours, we're headed to the tropics. Hawaii, to be exact. We've got a show dedicated to the sounds of sea breezes, chirpy birds, and clinking glasses: Martin Denny, Les Baxter, and more. So get out your bikini, Bermudas, or grass skirt. Put a log on the fire and mix yourself a drink. It's time for a luau, right here on Shaken, Not Stirred, Nebraska Public Radio.

NebraWeather

Ingrid owns the latest, most exclusive weather radio, a gift from Mario last spring. She loves it, but sometimes the computer-generated male voice issuing forecasts gets on her nerves.

An approaching winter storm may lead to blizzard conditions, with up to two feet of snow predicted for portions of southeast Nebraska and southwest Iowa by early tomorrow morning. Winds of up to 60 miles per hour in large swaths of treeless areas will result in drifting snow and closing of roads throughout the area. This is a fast-approaching storm, so citizens are urged to stock up on supplies immediately. School closures are expected for the first part of the week. Police and National Guard are on alert, and travelers are urged to find lodging immediately. Log onto Nebra-D-O-T dot com for the latest road conditions and stay tuned for any updates to your local forecast.

Mario's Phone Message on Ingrid's Machine

Ingrid's message machine is located on the second floor in the hallway outside the bedrooms.

The Hula DVD sounds fantastic, but I'm thinking we should skip our little Docu-Night, with the storm coming and all. The last thing we need is for your son and daughter-in-law to have an excuse to whisk you away to California because you had a mishap on the way to my place. We both know they think I'm a bad influence. Let's talk on the phone. The Hawaiian salad can keep, along with the DVD. Call when you get in, so I know you're okay. Bye for now.

Ingrid's Imagined Conversation with a Hawaiian

Although she retired from the library two years ago, Ingrid refuses to give up the idea of broadening other people's view of the world. Lately she has imagined herself speaking casually to interesting people in other places. This conversation occurs in the downstairs parlor, as the phone rings and Mario leaves his message.

Much of southeast Nebraska is anything but flat, and anyone who thinks so is as ignorant as a gathering of middle-aged *haoles* imitating the hula by shaking their hips and fanning their fingers. Just as Hawaii is more than tropical breezes, especially on the stinging or burning slopes of Mount Kilauea, Nebraska is more than flat farmlands. The southeastern quadrant of the state features straight rolling hills, tucked away colleges, and an abundance of trees along the Missouri. The best way to get the lay of the land is to use your imagination while moving your body. The first step is to picture a runner rug. Then sit down on the floor and slide your arms under the rug, perpendicular to the length of the runner. Lift your arms lightly, just a few inches, and then slide them back, making sure to leave the rug as it is. See the waves that formed from your arms? Up and down, up and down—all in a straight line. Very organized but gentle: sort of like the hula. Put some crops, trees, buildings, and cars on the runner-rug landscape, and you get southeast Nebraska.

No, it doesn't get lonely here. There are three ups and three downs between my house and my best friend Mario's. We live three miles apart. On nice days, when I visit him or he visits me, cars are left at home. Sometimes we get together and walk the trails at Arbor Day Farm, where you can get a free tree to plant. In winter, we get together once a week for Docu-Night, which consists of eating dinner while listening to music, watching a documentary, reading out loud, and participating in an activity that relates directly to the documentary.

Ingrid's Latest Health List

Four times a year, instead of going to the doctor, Ingrid makes health lists, both for her physical and mental health.

Plusses
1. memories of Hank
2. Mario's friendship
3. books and the library
4. learning
5. my home

Minuses
1. no money to travel
2. old age
3. Michael's reticence

4.   Nicole's influence

5.   loneliness

Decisions

1.   Save money for travel.

2.   Be myself at all times.

3.   Enjoy life.

Ingrid's Notes for Docu-Night

A lover of bullet points, Ingrid always writes reminder notes on the computer.

- Bring DVD, Hawaiian salad, hula book, hula doll, and CD of *Shaken, Not Stirred*.
- Remember to read quote from hula teacher Helen Desha Beamer: "Everything you feel must show in your whole being. If you're doing a hula about a person, you must study the person so well that you feel you know them. Your feelings must then show through so well in everything you do as you dance, that the audience feels it has experienced the presence of the person you are dancing about. It is the same when you dance about things of nature."
- Practice reach-tap hula step: put your right foot out front and your left hip up. Bring the foot back. Put your left foot out front and your right hip up. Bring the foot back. Repeat, allowing hips to swivel. Imagine flowering ohia tree when performing the steps.
- Memorize the following song lyrics from 1937 film *Waikiki Wedding*: *We should be together . . . in the little hula heaven over the silver sea. Gay and free together . . . in the little hula heaven under the koa tree.*
- Reread pages of hula text that document destruction of Hawaiian culture by Christian missionaries.

Ingrid's iPhone Video

Think of the word *trudge*—its definition and sound—and you can imagine the movements Ingrid makes, as she steps through a foot of newly fallen snow on her way from house to

49

barn. The iPhone shakes as she moves through the dark. The wind has yet to pick up, so the snow is still peaceful, flakes falling in unison, dotting the dark with the icy precision of a Russian ballerina. "Skol, says Ingrid," snapping a selfie, as her rectangular silhouette plods along. "I look like a block of ice. That's what happens when a 71-year-old puts on six layers and a backpack and goes out in the snow." Ingrid takes a deep breath. "Refreshing," she says, facing the screen of the phone. "I am on my way to a Hawaiian luau, Nebraska style, in January on a John Deere." A couple years before he died, Ingrid's husband Hank bought a snowplow—rigged it in place of the bucket on the front loader of an old tractor. "Too bad Willa's not still around Red Cloud," she says. "Could use me for a story. Boy, won't Mario be surprised when I show up at his house in this contraption."

The Breakdown

When the tractor-snowplow breaks down, Ingrid has only one up and one down before reaching the driveway of Mario's modest brick ranch. She turns on her iPhone, accesses her notes, and utters a line out of "Snow," a Canadian short story by Frederick Philip Grove: "The snow suddenly gave way beneath him; he broke in; the drift was hollow." She takes a breath. "That's how I feel around Nicole, even if it's 75 degrees in February. When that woman prays to her hateful god for the salvation of my soul, I feel as if I'm dropping into a cold, dried-up California canyon, faster and faster with every word she utters. Out here I'm alive. Hank's with me." Ingrid lowers herself from the tractor and raises her head. "I am on a mission to spread Hawaiian culture in southeast Nebraska," she shouts. As she walks up the third hill, the wind picks up, and the snow intensifies. Ingrid can no longer see the road.

Ingrid's List of Medications and Health Report

You can see a printed copy of this list on Ingrid's refrigerator. Although she doesn't like to take meds, she never fails to miss a dose.

1. Lisinopril: one 10-mg tablet once a day for high blood pressure
2. Fexofenadine HCl: one 180-mg caplet, as needed for allergies

in spring and fall

Only after Michael married Nicole did Ingrid begin to show signs of high blood pressure. She's been taking allergy medicine of one sort or another since she was a child. The last time she had a cold was in the summer of 1998. In 2006, she switched doctors because the one she had, ten years younger than she, had died.

Michael's Medications and Health Report

Unable to produce children thanks to an antifungal medication he took in his late teens, Michael consumes a combination of seventeen different pills, capsules, and liquids for a variety of ailments ranging from diabetes to warts. In addition, he's about twenty pounds overweight.

Telepathy

Ever since Michael first went to school, he and his mother have corresponded through telepathy—not often, but enough to remind the two that their relationship deviates from those of other mothers and sons. While this unusual practice often worked well, as in the case of Ingrid offering Michael a surge of praise when he was up at bat, or Michael providing Ingrid a serving of confidence when she baked cakes for competitions, the shared gift eventually went sour. During his teens and early twenties, Michael failed to appreciate telepathic messages from his mother assessing the women he dated. For the past year, Ingrid has resented the extrasensory suggestion that she move to California and join her son and daughter-in-law at church.

Nowadays both mother and son have trained themselves to ignore the *chatter* in their minds. When Ingrid falls in the snow halfway down the last hill, she feels little impact from Michael's mental picture of a blazing fireplace keeping his mother warm as she reads a good book on a snowy night.

When he calls her, the machine picks up. He hangs up and tries her cell. "I wonder why she doesn't answer," says Michael.

"Maybe she's out tobogganing," says Nicole. "You know your mother has yet to accept the fact that she's an adult." Michael turns to his wife. "And what are you acting like," he says, "when you say things like that?" When Michael calls Mario, Ingrid's friend says she probably decided to watch the hula documentary the two were planning to see, which means she turned off her phones. "I can just see her now," he says, "pausing every few moments to stand up and perform a new step." Michael clears his throat. "I don't think that's the case," he says. "That's not what I feel."

Nebraska Hula

"That was stupid," says Ingrid, rolling from her side to her knees to stand up after landing in a soft snow bank. "If I were paying attention, I could've avoided such clumsiness." When she steps on her right foot, she feels snow in her boot and sits down. In the midst of fixing her footwear, she feels dizzy and decides to take a few bites of Hawaiian salad to give her strength. The top section is already frozen. She checks her phone: no service. "This means I've got about a quarter mile left." Ingrid takes a deep breath and inches her way through the storm, which, according to the NebraWeather Report she heard before leaving, has caused a whiteout from Rulo to Nebraska City. Having suffered from hypothermia as a child when riding her bike through a thunderstorm, Ingrid realizes that the fall has given her limited time to reach shelter.

"Last thing I want is for Nicole to get the satisfaction of telling Michael, 'I told you so,' " says Ingrid. She tries jogging in place and realizes how tired she has become. "If only I could lie down for a few minutes." Looking for a place to settle, she remembers Rule No. 1 from *How to Stay Alive in the Elements*, checked out only six times since the library acquired it in 1986 and the county switched over to digital due dates in 2000: *When the cold gets under your skin, increase your heart rate.* She reaches her arms into the air. "Not until I've saved enough money to get to Hawaii and back am I ready to join you, Hank."

Thinking of the anniversary trip to Maui she and her husband had planned before his illness, Ingrid begins to perform the reach-tap hula step. Allowing her hips to swivel as her feet move in and out, she heads down the road, chanting, "*E Pele e Pele.*" Ingrid feels a spark of warmth enter through her abdomen, and she picks up speed. "Thank you, Volcano Goddess." Slowly making her way down the last hill, Ingrid imagines Mario taking her coat, chiding her for not staying in on a night like tonight. When she reaches a snowdrift blocking Mario's long driveway, she curses Pele.

Hawaiian Legend Ingrid Thinks of to Keep Warm

Having grown up in a household in which her mother read or told stories by heart, especially when the children were afraid or upset, Ingrid recently resumed the tradition, telling herself stories, sometimes out loud, but most often in her mind.

Drawn by the beat of hula drums on the distant isle of Kauai, the Hawaiian Goddess Pele allows her spirit to separate from her body, as she slumbers at the fiery bottom of Kilauea crater. When her spirit traverses the sea to the temple at Haena, Kauai, she falls in love with Chief Lohiau. Several days later, her spirit returns to her body quite suddenly. After she awakens, she asks her siblings to find the chief and bring him to her. Her hula-dancing sister Hiiaka agrees and sets forth on a long, death-defying journey, on which she battles a giant lizard, a shark-god, and a second giant lizard, whose tongue is disguised as a bridge over a deep mountain gorge. Free from monstrous creatures, Hiiaka runs into bad weather. By the time Hiiaka and Chief Lohiau return to Kilauea crater, Pele has given up and sought revenge by burying her sister's ohia trees and sacrificing on the altar of jealousy Hiiaka's friend and hula teacher Hopoe. Although the story originates from more than a thousand years ago, hula dancers continue to reenact its events.

Nebraska Pioneer Remedies

Why Ingrid thinks of these as she stands before a giant snowdrift, she is not sure.

- By carrying around a raw potato, sufferers of rheumatism allow the root vegetable to absorb the pain and cure the ailment.
- To cure warts, simply steal your neighbor's dishrag and destroy it.
- If you suffer from eczema, place a dozen pennies on the infected area for twenty-four hours, then wash thoroughly with vinegar.

Digging Deeper

According to Ingrid's estimate, the only way through to Mario's house is to enter the drift, at least six feet high and shaped like a volcano. Going around it would mean risking getting lost. Ingrid realizes she will need something to slice through the snow. Inside her backpack is a long metal serving spoon—Mario has yet to furnish his kitchen with adequate equipment. "Digging will make me warm," she says, "but I'll need to take breaks to preserve my heart." If she reaches high enough with the spoon, she can scoop off the top of the drift. Ingrid sets the timer on her iPhone. "I'll dig for three minutes and then write notes for one." During the first round of digging, she realizes her lips are beginning to freeze, so she pulls out her hula book, shines a flashlight on the first chapter, and sings the following chant:

> Look at the dancing girl Hopoe;
> Her graceful hips swing to and fro,
> A dance on the beach Nanahuki:
> A dance that is full of delight.
> Down by the sea Nanahuki.

The next time she runs out of steam, Ingrid copies down the aforementioned hula chant in the notes section of her iPhone, allowing her hips to shake as her thumbs punch out the words. "This way I won't destroy the book any more than I already have," she says, blowing on Pages 2 and 3 to minimize the possibility of water stains. She continues to dig. "Quarter of the way through," she says, not really sure if she's gotten that far. Her next set of notes chronicles the snippets of Nebraska folklore, followed by a statement that pioneer Nebraskans were no more or less superstitious than traditional Hawaiians. Her third note, also written on her iPhone, which still has no service, is a telepathic text to Michael: *Let go once in a while. Don't let Nicole spoil all your fun, as I once did.*

Ingrid's digging has caused her to sweat, the wind has slowed down, and the intensity of the snowfall has begun to diminish. She estimates she is halfway through the drift.

The Hula Doll

Although the temperature in Michael's house is 77 degrees—Nicole likes it warm—Michael feels cold. "Next week I'm going home for a visit," he says to his wife. "Alone." Nicole reminds her husband that the visit will have to come after the upcoming church revival, and Michael says, "To hell with the revival." Once Nicole has removed herself from the room and gone to bed, Michael gets out his diary. He writes the following: *I wonder what Mom's researching these days—the Amazon rainforest, nutrition in New Guinea, the invention of the bifocal? What novels are you reading? Books of poetry? Biographies? I'm sorry I never lived up to your imagination. You live in a library. I crunch numbers in an office building.*

Michael goes into his tiny California attic to look through boxes. After a few minutes, he discovers one of his old hula dolls—slender, the grass skirt tan, the halter top a pink paisley print. He places the doll on top of the box before him, reaches his arms to the left, and attempts to swivel his hips. His back locks. His body has become twisted, like a gnarled Nebraska oak.

Marva and Misha

When I was a girl, ballet was big. Baryshnikov defected from Russia, and mainstream America took notice. For once, ballet was more than *The Nutcracker,* tacky recitals, and the source of snide remarks about male homosexuality. Even my father the banker grew interested, when he heard about the Russian in Capezios darting through downtown Toronto, the KGB at his soft leather heels. Unfortunately, during the summer of '75, all I cared about was turning into a carbon copy of my friends. Three out of ten girls in my fifth-grade class in Shafton, Pennsylvania, took ballet lessons. This meant that I would drop dead if I didn't do exactly the same thing. That's what I told my parents, and they sort of believed me. Of course I had no real interest in ballet, other than getting swept off my feet by Misha—that's what ballet people call Baryshnikov right to this day, whether they know him or not.

Despite their wealth, my parents made a big deal about paying for ballet classes. It's not that they weren't generous; they just wanted me to appreciate the expense. Also, they liked to play poor in order to fit in. That's what you had to do to get along in Shafton. First the mines played out, then the factories. By the time I was a teen, we were down to one dress factory, which didn't last long. Referred to as a borough, not a town, Shafton had a population of 5,000 back then. Now they have less than half. The place has one traffic light and no sign of a mall. Between Johnstown and the West Virginia border, southwest PA is known for forested rolling ridges and fields of crops. It's a region where going out of town means going up a hill.

To say there was nothing to do is an understatement. Without dance, I don't know what I would have done. I went three times a week to a tiny ballet studio on the corner of Kelly and Pulaski. A partially converted bakery, the ballet school smelled more of bread and cookies than sweat and feet. About 40 and single, our teacher Miss Tilda lived upstairs, where she baked all kinds of goodies she sold to the IGA down the street. Round cheeks, ample breasts, and a jolly laugh made Miss Tilda look more like a baker than a ballet teacher. Of course she did her best and treated us all like the children she never had. Miss Tilda's Little Studio of Ballet: that's what she called it. Our teacher was never one to hide the fact that her performing arts establishment was rinky-dink—too small for anything serious. But classes were cheap, and no one cared. We spent most of the time giggling instead of dancing, so space was not really an issue.

We were quite settled in our routine. I stood between Chrissie and Julie, both intent upon adding disco moves to every combination at the barre. If you look at an old picture, we resembled a girls' version of *The Three Stooges*. Chrissie was tall and had wild, curly red hair; Julie was short and had a big J sewn on her leotard, not unlike the L for Laverne in the TV series *Laverne and Shirley*; and I was the one with eyeglasses and a loose bun on the back of my head—bobby pins littering the floor the more I bounced around. There were ten of us altogether. Then came a girl named Marva—long legs, good feet, and a thin frame. Showed up completely out of the blue on a Saturday in the middle of winter, 1976. Said she was going to be a ballerina. I looked at Marva, then at my friends, and we laughed, all except Marva. She was so serious standing there— lips taut, spine erect—when she said the word *ballerina*. I'll never forget that moment. It tells more about us than her. Busted for being ordinary: that's what we all were—too ordinary, in fact, to even know it.

One thing's for sure: thanks to Marva, the whole dynamic of Miss Tilda's morphed. When Marva danced, we all got quiet. Despite Miss Tilda's ineptness—she never danced professionally and relied heavily on some book to teach the class—the girl who wanted to be a ballerina truly showed talent. We couldn't help but look at her, wondering in astonishment. I guess when you come from a third-rate factory town, where Miss Tilda's glazed donuts rank highest when it comes to something elegant and refined, Marva's attitude was more than a little strange.

"Marvelous, Marva," Miss Tilda used to say at least three times a class. "I wish you girls would learn by example."

Marva made the rest of us look like bumbling buffoons,

which, I suppose, we were, and we reacted by giving her a hard time. Chrissie, on a regular basis, put Elmer's glue in Marva's ballet slippers, and Julie, whose parents let her watch grownup movies on TV, called Marva Marnie, after the character in the old Hitchcock thriller by the same name. Although Marva was blond like Tippi Hedren, who played the role of Marnie, that's where the resemblance ended. Marnie was a thief and a liar; Marva was the opposite. Both, however, had a far-off look in their eyes and hated the color red.

But no matter what we said or did, Marva was the perfect little ballerina: pleasant but distant, dedicated to her art. Even though we teased Marva and said we despised her, no one really did. Part of the reason was Miss Tilda, who got carried away on a regular basis and told Marvelous Marva to lead the pack in center-floor combinations that never changed—pivot slowly in *arabesque* for the adagio and *balancé balancé, glissade grand jeté* for the allegro. Funny thing, though: under such pressure, Marva always messed up, and we all laughed. While Marva held her head in shame as Miss Tilda tried to explain what to do, the rest of us softened. That's how we got to like the only child who said she wanted to be a ballerina.

One day when Marva and I were 12, she came into the studio with a box of kittens: mewing and shaking clumps of orange, white, and black, as cute as Misha was hot. Marva said her mother was allergic, and they all had to go. I fell in love with one that had orange markings and black stripes. It made me think of a miniature Bengal tiger. Unlike the others, the tiger cat was fearless. When Miss Tilda put on the music for jumps, the cat leaped out of the box and joined us in center floor. Immediately, I claimed the cat and named him Misha. Marva cried when I took Misha home. He was her favorite, too. I said she could come visit, and she did, nearly every weekend, for the rest of the year. That's how we became best friends.

In preparation for Marva's first appearance at our house, I went all out—borrowed my mother's makeup and made sure that Misha's bowl and bed were clean and fresh. But unlike my other friends, Marva had no interest in putting on rouge and mascara; instead, she wanted to go outside.

"Let's play defection," she said.

Of course I had no idea what she was talking about, but chose to be polite.

"I'll be Misha—the dancer, not the cat—and you can be the KGB," said Marva, her voice slow and methodic, as if her decision took great care, as if she were some casting director planning a re-creation of Baryshnikov's defection.

"What do I do?" I asked.

"Try to catch me," said Marva.

"Then what?"

"What do you mean, 'Then what?'" Marva's voice pulsed with indignation.

"What do I do if I catch you?"

"That will never happen."

The game turned into an endless chase that burned off calories from the doughnuts I often swiped from Miss Tilda's kitchen. And no matter how hard I tried, I couldn't catch the aspiring ballerina *grand jetéing* over sidewalk puddles, darting behind parked cars, and crouching until I was a block away and out of breath. In addition to my limited level of fitness, I had a handicap: Marva forced me to run in a pair of oversized boots she picked up at a second-hand store and painted red to represent the Communists. When the boots didn't fit, she stuffed them with paper money from my brother's Monopoly game. I was lucky I didn't break an ankle. The one time Marva assumed the role of the KGB, she purposely let me win. When I asked why, she said she wasn't very good at playing anything other than a world-class professional ballet dancer.

When the weather became too cold or rainy for our game of chase, we played another game, rendered from Marva's obsession with ballet, alongside her limitless imagination. From her picture book of famous ballet dancers she chose a photo and taught me to act out the pose in the picture. Her favorite pose was one of Baryshnikov and Alla Sizova, both at the apex of a leap, performing starring roles in the ballet *Giselle*. That's the story about a young maiden who goes crazy and kills herself with her suitor's sword after he jilts her. In the picture, Baryshnikov and his partner are smiling, his right hand skimming her left. The first time I saw it, my eyes went straight to Misha's bulge, while Marva attempted to recreate the scene. Unlike Miss Tilda, Marva was a taskmaster. She wouldn't give up till I was dripping with sweat, trying to imitate the leap—a *grand jeté*, front leg straight, back leg bent. With every attempt, my dancing worsened. Either I ended up on the wrong leg, or the leg that was supposed to be straight ended up bent or the bent one straight. Taking on the persona of a great choreographer—Diaghilev one moment, Balanchine the next—Marva waved her arms and shouted, telling me to get my act together, or I could spend the rest of my life "in the back of the corps, never to perform a solo or principal role again." We ended up rolling on the ground, tears streaming from our eyes we were laughing so hard. My kid brother called us nuts.

Not long after Julie, Chrissie, and I turned 14—Marva was a few months younger—ballet suddenly got harder. The three of us grew boobs and couldn't keep our balance. So, we quit, altogether. Marva, who was busy taking ballet from a private teacher twenty miles away, grew taller but not too big. A recruiter from a dance conservatory in Connecticut held an audition in Johnstown and invited Marva to study with a full scholarship. Soon after, Marva invited me home for the first time. A tar-papered bungalow on the wrong side of the tracks, her house was spotless and sparse—no television, no dishwasher, no dryer. Yet the living room had floor-to-ceiling shelves filled with books. We went right to Marva's tiny bedroom, where we sat on the floor and spoke quietly.

"I can't go," said Marva, her voice trembling. "The scholarship covers tuition, not room and board."

"Can't your parents pay?" I asked.

Marva shook her head. "They can't afford it."

I offered to ask my parents for money, and Marva said she already thought of that, but her parents would never take charity. Just as I suggested a loan from my father's bank, Marva's mother knocked on the door.

A short, thin woman with a long gray braid, Marva's mother stepped lightly into the room, as if her entry were an apology. She wore a battered pair of bedroom slippers with a tiny hole exposing her left big toe. Marva introduced me, and her mother told me she had overheard our conversation.

"I don't mean to pry," she said, "but you have to understand that my husband is Ukrainian, a very proud man. Above all, he is against Communism. A scholarship is one thing, but taking money from others, even if they are rich, is another. To him, it's Communism, the one thing he escaped when he came to this country."

"But he could pay back the loan," I said.

"It won't work," said Marva.

"Thank you for understanding," said her mother, looking first at her daughter, and then at me, before tiptoeing out of the room.

Marva suggested we go outside, but I protested. My mind was jumping around, as if it were performing an *échappé*, legs going in opposite directions simultaneously, as the dancer jumps from fifth to second position and back again. Everything I could think of seemed to fall into the category of Communism, as defined by Marva's father. The feeling was strange.

"How much do you need?" I asked.

"Five thousand dollars," said Marva.

"What if you worked for it? Would your father approve?"

"Of course, but how am I going to do that?"

I didn't have the answer but knew someone who might: Miss Tilda. On our way to see our old ballet teacher, I looked at Marva and tried to figure out why she couldn't be like the rest of us. She was an only child, and her father was an immigrant, but that didn't explain why she had to be a ballerina.

"How did you get interested in dance?" I asked, as we walked past the IGA.

"My father," said Marva. "On Friday nights, after he has a tiny glass of vodka, he puts on a record of Ukrainian folk music and dances."

"Folk dancing?" I said, trying to imagine a Ukrainian version of the do-si-do.

"The most amazing acrobatics you've ever seen," said Marva, beginning to sound like her old self. "He crouches in a deep plié and goes running across the floor, his legs kicking up and out.

When he gets up, he does split jumps. My mother and I laugh and cheer him on."

"So why didn't you study Ukrainian dance?" I asked.

"My parents have a picture book of ballet dancers," she said, almost in a whisper. "I've been looking at it since I was four. Ballet is what I want to do."

"But why?"

"I can't really explain it, but when I dance, something happens, deep inside. My whole body feels like it's singing in church, when the choir and organ fill the sanctuary; everything becomes one. Dance is something I have to do."

"Oh," I said.

Miss Tilda was happy to see us. When I brought her up to speed on Marva's father's philosophy, the ballet teacher suggested we put on a father-daughter show and charge money, but Marva said her father never danced in public. Then I came up with an idea: to go around town and speak to all the merchants who belong to the chamber of commerce, tell them Marva will model, advertise their products, and dance at their office parties, if they invest in her future.

"We can say, 'Marva is the one hope we have to put Shafton on the map.' "

"Yes," shouted Miss Tilda. "And we can take pictures of Marva dancing in front of each of the businesses we approach."

"It feels like we're inside one of those old musicals," said Marva, "where they do a show about putting on a show. It's too corny. It'll never work."

Miss Tilda took Marva's hands. "Here's my contribution to corny, so listen carefully. You'll never know unless you try."

Marva practiced on Miss Tilda, who offered her $100 to clean her studio once a week for a month.

As long as Marva was working for money, her father was happy. With only two months to get the $5,000, we decided to start big: the owner of the dress factory, an old man living alone in Shafton's only mansion—white pillars, big front porch, and a slate roof, the shingles imported from Wales. My mother had nicknamed him Scrooge and told us we were wasting our time. We didn't dare tell Marva's father we were going to see the big

62

boss. Miss Tilda, who drove us and waited in the car, reminded us that even Ebenezer Scrooge could be reformed. It was 10 a.m. on a weekday when Marva and I rang Scrooge's bell, both of our hands pressing the gold button for good luck. After a very long minute, we were greeted by the snap of an upstairs window.

"This better be good," said the dress factory owner, leaning out, half of his face covered in shaving cream and the other half decorated in scowl lines and a trickle of blood.

"Forget it," said Marva. "We made a mistake."

"That I don't doubt," said the factory owner. "But don't think you're getting away so fast. I want to know who you are, what you want, and who put you up to this."

Marva stepped forward and set her "gaze to the balcony," as Miss Tilda used to say. "I'm nobody, I'm looking for scholarship money, and no one put me up to this."

"Scholarship money for what?"

"Ballet training in Connecticut."

The man let out a laugh that quickly turned into a cough.

"Let's just go," I said.

"You with the tits," said the man, pointing at me. "Good idea. And don't let me see either of you ever again."

This was the only time I beat Marva in a race. I was crouched in the back seat, tears streaming down my face, at least five seconds before Marva entered the car.

"What are *you* crying about?" she said. "At least the idiot didn't drip blood on your head."

Marva sounded so much like me that I stopped crying. Then Miss Tilda gave us a pep talk, and we headed to the IGA. Unlike the factory owner, the storeowner was happy to speak with us. He, along with the bakery manager, who raved about Miss Tilda's donuts, gave Marva cash donations—$30 altogether. Mr. Oskovich at the laundromat gave us $15. Julie and Chrissie's parents, also store owners, each gave $50. After two weeks of beating the pavement, we had $304, blisters on our feet, and solid evidence that most of the prominent residents of Shafton had little interest in ballet or the betterment of our youth.

A week before the two months were up, my brother suggested we try the owner of the movie theater. It was during

Sunday dinner. My mother had made a pot roast.

"Have you met this guy?" I asked.

"Not yet," said my brother, who had lived at the movie theater on Saturday afternoons, when I was at ballet. "But I've seen him. He's always got a flashlight. Shines it on high-school kids sitting in the back. Trying to catch them making out."

"Spoiling all the fun," joked my father.

"Quit that," said my mother. "I've seen that man around town. He has a suspicious-looking face, if you ask me."

My father asked my mother to lay off, and Marva and I set up a plan. This time she would come prepared. Underneath her jeans and T-shirt, she would wear a leotard and tights. If the theater owner could experience her talent firsthand, then he couldn't refuse. A short, ruddy-faced man with a balding head and long sideburns, the owner listened to our spiel for a minute, before inviting us to see a movie for free.

"We'll talk after I close up," he said, "if you're willing to wait."

We were. The theater closed at five on Sundays, right after the next film.

We both went out to talk to Miss Tilda. She insisted on coming in, but I asked her not to.

"The man keeps a picture of himself standing with his wife and two daughters right on the lobby wall for everybody to see," I said. "We'll be fine. Come back for us after the movie."

"If you're not out by five-twenty," said Miss Tilda, "I'm coming in."

"I appreciate what you're doing," said Marva.

Miss Tilda told us to insist on meeting in the lobby, especially since it was the only space big enough for Marva to perform. The movie was so boring I can't even remember the name of it. Marva spent half the time in the bathroom. At ten after five, we stood impatiently on the red, drink-stained carpet of the lobby, waiting for the last of the theatergoers and work crew to leave.

"I don't know about this," said Marva.

"This is our last chance," I said, reminding her that lots of people came to the movies, which meant that business was good. "This man has money."

"But why does the carpet have to be red?" said Marva. "I feel like I just walked into a Hitchcock film."

"Want me to call you Marnie?" I joked.

The theater owner made an entrance. While Marva stripped down to her leotard and tights, I raved about her talents as a ballerina. Without music, she performed an excerpt from the Mirliton variation from *The Nutcracker,* which was no easy task on sticky carpet. Halfway through the variation I got a funny feeling and shifted my gaze from Marva to the theater owner. Behind his bushy eyebrows, the middle-aged man leered at Marva. Where his upper and lower lips connected, white beads of saliva bubbled over. A crooked smile crept onto the man's face. Three-fourths of the way through the variation, I stood before Marva, drew my right hand across my neck, and mouthed the word *cut.* Unfortunately, she was in another world. Seconds after she finished the variation, Marva and the theater owner headed to his office. I was told to wait in the lobby. When I tried the office door, it was locked. Then came a scream—Marva's—and following that, a yelp from the theater owner. Apparently, he had underestimated a kick between the legs from an aspiring ballerina. This time, Marva was in the car before I was out the door.

The following day I couldn't eat. Everything, including my stomach, felt brittle, as if I would break into a million pieces. I had let down my only real friend. I had misled her into thinking I could help, when all I could do was get us both in a bunch of trouble. Knowing that something major was wrong, Misha the cat stuck close to me that day, and when Marva came over, he sat quietly in her lap, refusing to play no matter how many cat toys I waved in front of him. After quizzing Marva about her scholarship offer, I found myself calling information for Connecticut. After waiting on hold, I asked if there was some way that the ballet conservatory could make an exception and grant enough money for Marva to stay the year. I remember Marva wildly imitating my pantomime to say, "Cut," but I ignored her. When I was told that "the conservatory has a special policy strictly limiting scholarships," I asked to speak to the director. My voice was low and very adult-like. Marva left the room. When the director identified herself, I cleared my throat and said the following:

"For the last two weeks, Marva Tchevchenko, one of the most talented dancers on the planet, risked her life trying to raise five . . . thousand . . . dollars to be at your school. In addition to talking to almost a hundred people looking for a sponsor, she was bled upon by an ugly old miser and nearly got raped by a sick theater owner. And if that's not the sort of dedication you're looking for, then you can all go to hell, the whole goddamned lot of you."

Failing to wait for a response, I hung up the phone. Marva went home, and for the rest of the afternoon I cried in my room. That evening, we received a knock at the door.

"I want to speak to girl who raise five *tousand* dollar from one telephone call," said Marva's father, giving his daughter a hug and a kiss at our doorstep. "My Marva is going to dance."

A Professional Male Ballet Dancer in Twelve Steps

Step 1: At the age of 5, find a special secret place where everything is good.

Your mommy and daddy are yelling again. Something about money. You know that money is made of paper, and paper comes from trees. Walk softly into the living room and look at the painting—so quiet and beautiful. See the big trees with orange, red, and yellow leaves? The painting reminds you of the picnic, the woods where you and your mother and father sat beside fallen colored leaves. Things were good. When you got home, your parents took the leaves you collected and ironed them between pieces of waxed paper. You said you loved the smell. Daddy said you were smelling hot leaves, and Mommy told you to be careful and not come too close to the iron. Your mother and father were nice to each other, weren't they? That was in the fall.

Now it's winter. The leaves are all brown. There's a bit of snow on the ground, but it's brown, too. You look at the ironed leaves, but that's not good enough. Nothing makes the yelling go away. You have to get inside the painting to do that. Look at the path between the trees—right there, where it's yellow on the ground. Get ready. Now spin around as fast as you can. No, that's not quite right. You have to take lots of little steps as you spin. That's better. Now do it faster. See how all the colors come together? You spin so hard you fall down. You get up and try again. When you spin hard and fast enough, you fall down, hit your head, and see stars. The yelling goes away for a second. When it comes back, close your eyes. When you open them, you'll be inside the painting. Practice going in and out. Learn the exact steps to take, so you can teach them to Mommy and Daddy. Then you can bring them. You can take a picnic, sit next to the colored leaves. No one will yell.

When trying to spin, you fall and hurt your head on the

coffee table, and your parents stop yelling. When the tears and blood are gone, they ask what you were doing. You say nothing. They ask again, and you show them your turns. They go away. You stand outside the closed bedroom door but can't hear what they say. When they come out, they ask if you want to learn how to dance? You say yes.

Step 2: Get used to the words *faggot* and *fag*.

You're 8 years old, riding on the school bus, and someone grabs your knapsack. Out go the ballet slippers: white Sanshas, split sole, elastics sewn across the tops in an X pattern to support your arches. Look at the little faggot ballerina, somebody shouts. One slipper flies over your head. Twinkle toes, do you dance on the tips of your toes? You try to catch it. Hey, faggot ballerina, are you a girl? Your father paid a lot for those shoes; you can't lose them. Give that back! you yell. Oh, the little fag finally talks. Someone has ripped off the elastics your mother stayed up so late to sew.

Step 3: Discover that the more you dance, the less you are liked.

You have one friend in fourth grade. His name is Brearly. You throw a ball to Brearly at recess, and he pushes it away. The other kids are starting to make fun of me, says Brearly. I can't be your friend anymore, not if you take ballet. You follow your mother's advice and ignore Brearly's comments. You decide to keep dancing and give up your friendship.

You've had no friends for three months. In an act of desperation, you throw yourself into a perfect side split. For a brief time, you're popular. Hey, let's play with Gumby's legs. You stand against the green cinderblock wall in Ms. Garggan's classroom, while big John Sunniti picks up your foot—your knees are both straight—and places it over your head and against the wall. Some of the girls let out a gasp. You feel satisfaction. On your way into the cloakroom, John Sunniti trips you. You fall. Three of John Sunniti's friends—Bobby Vaughan, Maxie Cooper, and Evan Pablitski—make it a habit to trip, push, and tease you at least twice a day. Ms. Garggan never seems to be around when things happen. When you get home after ballet, you take off your clothes and look at yourself in the mirror. Your legs are getting bigger. The next time Bobby, Maxie, and Evan try to trip you, your legs kick. It's as if they have a mind of their own. You don't stop until the three, all a lot bigger than you, are lying on the floor crying. You look at Bobby and Maxie and Evan and feel confused. Having learned that faggots are boys who like boys the way boys are supposed to like girls, you wonder why they think of you as a faggot, when all you feel for other boys is hate.

Step 4: Get used to your body.

At 15, you can no longer fit into any of your pants, thanks to the legs you've developed from dancing. Your mother takes you to the best department store in town. When you come out of the dressing room, thighs bulging through a pair of Ralph Laurens you hold up with your hands because the waist is too big, the clerk asks what sport you play. You tell him you are a dancer, and he says nothing. You try Dockers and Kenneth Coles, but to no avail. Your mother purchases one of each and takes you to the tailor.

All you do is walk into a room, and people get uncomfortable or act strange. When you catch them staring, you turn away. It's only getting worse as you get older. Some woman follows you down the bike trail and asks you out to Starbucks. You tell her your age, and she claims you are too muscular to be so young. When you tell her to go away, she accuses you of taking steroids. You tell her that's a lie. A girl at school says that male ballet dancers are all gay; anyone can tell from their butts, which are big. Gay ballet dancers with big butts get AIDS, she says. You hereby solemnly swear that you are asexual and will never have sex with a woman or a man.

Step 5: Leave home at 16 to study at the School of American Ballet in New York.

Floor-to-ceiling mirrors, barres attached to the walls, and enough space for twenty students to move and not get into each other's way. A far cry from the studio back home. Here you're no longer the only boy or the best dancer. You need to catch up. You have lots to do just to get good. Focus. Your teachers like you. Your parents come for a visit—to see how you're doing, to watch you perform the role of the jealous boyfriend in *Pastorale*. You chase and toss your partner around the stage. You neither like nor dislike her, so you work hard to convince your audience that you have a violent streak. You succeed by thinking of the times your parents fought. The applause is fantastic. Your parents commend you. During a special dinner at the Tavern on the Green, they let you know how much they love and support you. No football player can do what you do, says your father. You thank him. Is there anyone special in your life? asks your mother. You say no, and your father tells you not to worry if you are gay. You shake your head and ask how things are at home. Your parents say that everything's fine.

Step 6: Worship and pray.

You worship ballet through your allegiance to George Balanchine, one of the founders of the School of American Ballet and the artistic director of the New York City Ballet until his death. You credit the director, also a famous choreographer, as the originator of a distinctly American form of dance that celebrates individuality over uniformity and incorporates jazz, modern, tap, contra, and other dance forms associated with the states. You defend Balanchine when others fail to recognize his genius and accuse him of despotism. You believe that these people are un-American and should be investigated by the Department of Homeland Security.

> Every night you say the following prayer:
> *Our Ballet, Who art in motion,*
> *Corporeal be Thy Name;*
> *Thy Terpsichore come,*
> *Thy will be done,*
> *in studio as it is on stage.*
> *Give us this day, our daily class,*
> *and forgive us our missteps*
> *as we forgive those who misstep around us;*
> *and lead us not into relaxation,*

but deliver us from disorder,
Merde.

Merde is what you say instead of good luck, or, God forbid, break a leg, to a dancer about to perform. It's French and means shit.

Step 7: Accept and embrace contradiction.

You've made it—not New York City Ballet, but a City Ballet spinoff company in the Midwest. The director, a former principal with Balanchine's company, came to watch Men's Advanced. After class, he offered you a contract. You move to Missouri: fancy suburbs, rolling hills, and strong support for the ballet. You're about to perform your first full *pas de deux*—just what you've wished for. The curtain is about to go up, and the director is talking to his dancers. After whispering something into your partner's ear, he turns to you. Those thighs look kinda big in white tights, he says. You say nothing—too confused to understand whether he wants you to succeed or fail. During your solo you think back to rehearsal, when the director told you to imagine your legs as scissors cutting through the air. For a moment you think of Evan, Bobby, and Maxie, how they used to taunt you. When you jump, beating your legs back and forth in a movement called an *entrechat six,* you picture yourself as a pair of scissors, decapitating the director. You and your partner receive a standing ovation. The director says nothing.

Step 8: Profess your sexuality and act upon it.

The gay men in the company give up on trying to seduce you. You begin to comprehend your sexual orientation during a rehearsal for Balanchine's *Valse Fantaisie.* One man—that's you—and a bevy of ballerinas. You dance with each but feel nothing for any of them. The director bitches at you for not emoting. You try your best. When you get to the solo that ends with pirouettes—multiple turns executed while standing on the ball of one foot—you feel a sudden burst of energy from deep in your chest. You realize that you have fallen in love with turning. You revel in balancing on one leg and whipping around like a corkscrew. Nothing else gives you so much excitement, peace, and happiness. You feel relieved, having known all along that you were never meant to be intimate with another human being. When you turn, you leave the earth and enter heaven. Dance is your religion, pirouettes, your lover. You honor your lover, your country, and yourself by performing Balanchine's choreography. Just talking about turning makes you feel like you're headed to the top of a rollercoaster. The more turns the better. Turning is sex and a whole lot more. It starts in the ballet studio or on stage and lasts until you lie in bed naked, touching nothing; that's when you finally let loose. After a show, you get home, take a shower, get into bed, and close your eyes. Then, lying still, you reenact the time you danced right through the tornado sirens, not long after you joined the company. The sky turned green, and a funnel-shaped tail dipped down from the clouds. Your stomach fluttered. The director ordered you down to the basement. You looked at him and kept dancing. He told you to suit yourself. The tornado hit—knocked part of the roof in. You were turning when it happened. You relive these moments every night.

Step 9: Stay out of politics; relinquish your right to vote.

This is an extremely wise and insightful move because it serves as evidence that you are training yourself to deny democracy, which does not exist in any successful ballet studio or company. Think dictatorship. The artistic director is king or queen, or, in the case of your ballet company, both. If you obey the dictator, you may succeed; if not, you won't. Never join a group of dancers attempting to improve working conditions. If it's cold, put on a sweater. If it's wet, slip into a pair of plastic pants. Accept your place as a peon and do everything in your power to persuade the dictator to make you into a star. If you happen to be accepted into an AGMA ballet company, pay your dues, smile, and stretch your hamstrings during union meetings.

If you really want to play the role of the Prince in *Sleeping Beauty*, refrain from envisioning a world in which humans are created equal. If you wish to become royalty, you must accept the monarchy. Without Louis XIV, ballet would fail to exist. The very essence of ballet lies in the French king's royal desire to create a method of movement that would show off the definition of his calf muscles. You must honor the king.

Classical ballet celebrates class distinction. The best dancers do not waste their time thinking about human rights. Instead, they focus on allowing their bodies and minds to be used for higher purposes by directors, choreographers, and others in charge. Twentieth-century composer Igor Stravinsky, when working with Balanchine, put it best: He referred to dancers as pigs snouting [sic] mushrooms.

Step 10: Develop a working relationship with physical pain.

If you are to achieve long-term success as a professional male ballet dancer, you must accept and endure physical pain. Whether you know it or not, physical pain lives inside, outside, and all around you. Unless you go through physical pain, and physical pain goes through you, you will not succeed as a professional. Physical pain pushes, pulls, throbs, burns, stings, stabs, penetrates, and emasculates. Feel it riding your nerves like a racecar on a track. You can't escape physical pain. It thrives in beauty. When the audience gasps with pleasure as you perform a powerful press lift, it is physical pain that sees you through. You listen to it.

Stand directly behind your dance partner. Place your hands on either side of her lower back. Your knees are bent. In one powerful count, straighten your knees and arms, lifting your partner high above your head, causing your spine to bend backward as you turn her in a circle. Feel that piercing shimmer in your skeleton, like a wave full of sand scraping your spine? That's physical pain. Feel that throb pulsating between your biceps and shoulders, like rats gnawing on your muscles? There it is again. You are grateful for physical pain because you're willing to do whatever it takes, feel whatever is necessary to truly dance.

Step 11: Meet injury.

You're turning. Subtle as a pinprick, physical pain enters your left foot, causing your cuboid to split ever so slightly. The hairline fracture gives your foot just enough extra width to execute six flawless pirouettes—slicing windmills, perfect in their uniformity—no hopping, no falling in one direction or the next after the fourth or fifth. The pain increases as you practice, from pin jabs to piercing needles. Physical pain begets injury. The sensation the injury gives you is what enables you to do the turns. Yes, you can mask physical pain with drugs, but the injury will not go away. You get used to the injury roaming around, reshaping your foot. You get the part: Don Quixote. Your dancing has never been better. The pleasure the injury allows you is so great, you don't need painkillers. You no longer feel the presence of physical pain. As long as you don't deny the injury, as well as the pain that brought it on, you'll be fine. Before the season's over, physical pain will resurface, and you'll feel it enough to take time off, let the injury run its course. Acknowledge the injury with reverence, and it will let up. The stress fracture will heal. Any male dancer worth the salt of his sweat knows, feels, respects, and acknowledges his relationship with injury.

Step 12: At the age of 20, face what hurts the most and keep dancing.

Although your foot is injured, you still must dedicate yourself to pirouettes. You find a way of doing it without dancing every minute; the stress fracture has to heal. As soon as the season ends, you go storm chasing in Oklahoma. As you're driving you see funnels coming toward you from three directions. The sky reminds you of your grandmother's health drink—avocados and carrot juice whirling around in the blender. You remember the summer you stayed at her house, worked in her garden. She told you to eat well and ignore the crap. You stop the car on the side of the road. No one is around. The air is heavy and textured. You try a few turns *à la seconde* as the lightning dances above your head.

The rain begins, and your foot starts to throb. You let yourself feel the pain. It reminds you of nettles, stinging your skin as you played barefoot around your grandmother's brook. You get back in the car and head in the one direction you don't see funnels. You find shelter at the Y, next to a mother and father, holding their young son. Around the eyes, the boy looks a bit like Brearly. When the storm passes over, you get back in your car and stay overnight at a cheap motel. You dream of dancing in the middle of a tornado's funnel. The experience is shockingly boring. You feel nothing from turning. When you wake up, you drive a few miles—past the remnants of a town demolished by a rotating force you thought you understood. You stop at a diner and fill up on bacon, eggs, and biscuits. You chat with the waitress, who wears a yellowish scar above her left eyebrow—a reminder, she says, of the last tornado that ripped through town. Her hips are wide, and she walks with her head down and shoulders concave. Her irises make you think of fallen leaves, after the colors are gone. She's probably never even heard of ballet. You like her. More biscuits? she asks. You look like you could use it. Sure, you say, why not? Come down from the city to help out? No—just passing through.

You use your muscles and strength to lift fallen beams, dig through the rubble of a demolished school. You recover a dead child, a boy, probably around 5. His arms are reaching up, hands splayed, not unlike a pose from Balanchine's *Agon*. A woman comes running. That's my son, she says. She grabs the corpse and kisses it, begging God to let the boy wake up. When he doesn't, the woman throws up on your feet. When you return home, you go to physical therapy three times a week for your injury. As the therapist massages your foot, you get a call from your mother. She asks how you're doing, says she saw on the news that people were killed in a series of tornadoes. You tell your mother you met a nice woman, a waitress with brown eyes. She says, That's wonderful. When the therapist packs your foot in ice, you turn off your phone and think about the upcoming season, what you will dance next.

The Dancing Bee

Unlike Mr. Soren's other piano students, James has the gift of perfect pitch, yet he rarely practices or looks at the sheet music. Every time he hits a wrong note, he tilts his head and smiles. This repeated action gives the impression that when he plays, he's having the time of his life—head bobbing right to left, lips stretching like cherry bubblegum ready to snap. A month ago, when James turned 14, he started working on "The Busy Bee," a song that 9-year-old Carol Morris mastered in a week.

"You know that bees do a dance?" says James, suddenly stopping in the middle of his lesson. "Found out in science class. They shake their bodies like crazy to tell the other bees where the nectar is hiding." The boy's speech accelerates. "It's called the waggle dance: what the bees do. The scout bees waggle around in a figure eight. How the figure eight is performed is based on the distance between the hive and the flowers. Isn't that cool? If it wasn't for the dancing bees, the other bees wouldn't know where to go or how to get there."

Mr. Soren taps his hands on the side of the instrument. "And where, James, are you going, carrying on a conversation, when you're supposed to be playing the piano?"

"Okay, okay. I just thought you might want to know."

"Thank you for telling me. You're a smart boy. Now how about waggling your fingers on the keys. All right, James?"

"But bees are so interesting."

"Okay," says Mr. Soren, accentuating the wrinkles in his forehead as he raises his eyebrows. "Think of your right hand as five busy dancing bees—a finger for each."

James shakes his head, his long curly hair landing between his eyes. "Male bees don't dance. All they do is have sex with the queen."

Mr. Soren stands up, reaches over James's shoulders, and plays the opening of "The Busy Bee," saying the notes as he presses the keys: "GFED, FEDC, GFED, FEDC. How simple is that?" Accidentally grazing the boy's head with his chin, he pulls back. A flash of sciatica shimmers through his left leg.

James stumbles through the right notes without any recognition of timing. The song sounds like an old car that can't start.

"Your hour's up a bit early," says Mr. Soren. "I think we've both had enough."

"Enough of what?" says James.

Mr. Soren looks the boy in the eye. "James, if you don't practice, there's no sense in playing. Are you sure you want to continue with the piano?"

"I *love* coming here," says James, his voice beginning to crack.

"Then practice," says Mr. Soren.

James makes a buzzing sound while shaking his buttocks, before scampering down the steps of the old Victorian.

"Please, no running in or around the premises," says Mr. Soren, his oversized Adam's apple bobbing up and down. "The house is getting old, just like your teacher. We can't take it."

"Sorry."

Insisting that his pupils address him by surname, Mr. John Soren lives alone in a two-story Queen Anne with gingerbread latticework, loud ticking clocks, and a porthole window in the turret. He inherited the house from his Aunt Melody, who died last year at 90. Both of his parents passed when he was a toddler, and his single aunt raised him without help. When he first entered kindergarten, Johnny Plebbete—Mr. Soren's name until he found out that the term *pleb* denotes commonality, and *bête* means *stupid* in French—told the teacher he could learn nothing surrounded by mere children. After completing a bachelor's degree in piano performance, he changed his name and settled on a 30-year career selling musical instruments. Playing in front of people had made him too nervous.

Still sporting a thick head of black hair, not dyed, Mr. Soren is now 60. On the street, when he walks from his house to the old soda fountain for a root beer float, he could pass for 49. With a long neck and honey-smooth skin, the fifth generation Midwesterner has good genes. Thanks to a sizable inheritance, he also has plenty of money. The few dollars he earns from teaching piano, he donates to charity.

James is his last student of the week. Five minutes after the boy has begun his walk home, Mr. Soren heads out back, if the weather is nice. Surrounded by a tall, thick fortress of hedges, the space is large and secluded. A little after four, in the first part of September, a wedge of sun shines right between the buttocks of Mr. Soren's cherub, a nineteenth-century fountain Aunt Melody had picked up in the Pyrenees. With his lime green yoga mat and a glass of iced tea made from homegrown mint, Mr. Soren makes his way down the brick walkway. After placing his tea on a small wrought-iron table, he peels off his clothes and places them neatly on the back of a matching chair. He sets up his mat a few feet from the cherub, whose open mouth emits an arc of water into a shallow pool. When the breeze picks up, the fountain sounds as if it's whispering, "What are you doing? What are you doing? What are you doing?"—one sentence mellifluously overlapping the next.

Since his aunt's death, Mr. Soren's sunny afternoon ritual has gone virtually unchanged during the month of September. He sits on his mat and sips tea for about ten minutes. Then he goes inside for a bathroom break, enjoying his nakedness as he walks. When he returns, he practices a variety of modern dance moves and yoga poses, which calm his nerves and keep him trim. Then he lies flat on his back and takes a nap, relying on his growling stomach to wake him in time to make dinner. On Fridays, he cooks a pork roast.

Despite the ample sunshine and low humidity, Mr. Soren feels out of sorts after James's lesson. He imagines the boy making fun of him—telling his family and friends about the strange old man fixated on fingering and timing and preserving his strange old house. A few years ago, the mother of another student accused the piano teacher of being out of touch with reality because he had told her daughter to practice her fingering in front of a mirror. Mr. Soren takes several deep breaths. The breeze picks up, and the fountain begins to whisper. Not until he has completed sixteen sun salutations does Mr. Soren begin to relax and enjoy the sounds of the birds. The goldenrod—his favorite flower—is reaching its peak. His next-door neighbor, who used to keep bees, hates the bright yellow blossom, says its nectar reeks like a men's locker room.

When Mr. Soren was James's age, a boy at school surprised him with a bouquet of goldenrods. He accepted the flowers and then hid them in his knapsack. The boy, frail and much smaller than others his age, was found beaten and unconscious in the gym locker room later that day. The next day, a group of popular boys recounted the incident with delight. They said that Johnny Plebbete was "next in line." The principal failed to discipline the boys, and Aunt Melody took her nephew out of school before anyone had a chance to hurt him. Until college, Johnny received the rest of his education at home. Never married, he keeps some of those flowers pressed in an old diary.

Facing the unobstructed September sky, Mr. Soren closes his eyes. Sleep comes almost simultaneously. He dreams of a honeybee dancing above the tip of his long but diminutive nose, the only body part that still earns him compliments. He lifts his hand to swat the bee. A moment later, hundreds of bees circle his head. Mr. Soren forces himself to stay still. The buzzing grows unbearable. In the background, he hears James's laughter. Mr. Soren awakens with a gasp. A honeybee buzzes by the head of the cherub. The piano teacher picks up his things and runs inside.

The dream repeats itself for the next three nights, the honeybees increasing in number, and James's voice growing shriller in each successive nightmare. The fact that the bees fail to sting makes Mr. Soren even more uptight, as he anticipates the pain. Sweating profusely, he goes through two pairs of pajamas a night. Getting back to sleep becomes nearly impossible. On the fourth night, after the dream, he goes looking for something to read. In his aunt's credenza, he comes across the old diary with the pressed goldenrods. He puts them back and goes to sleep.

* * *

During his next lesson, James gives Mr. Soren a surprise: For once the boy has practiced. "The Busy Bee" sounds the way it's supposed to—a simple melody, more of an exercise than a song. It's time to assign James something more difficult, a song that integrates both hands.

"How about 'The Flight of the Bumblebee'?" asks James.

"Too advanced," says Mr. Soren. "What's with you and bees?"

"I just think they're cool. Ever lie still and let one buzz around your face?"

"No," snaps Mr. Soren, thinking about his dream and then ripping open the sheet music to "The Cradle Song," by Johannes Brahms.

"I was just asking."

After James's lesson, Mr. Soren goes to the library and checks out two books on bees. From the first, he learns that James is correct about the waggle dance. From the second, he learns about the medieval tradition of "telling the bees" when a person is dead, to assure that the "spirit land" will be prepared for the new arrival. As the providers of the sacred mead or honey wine, bees were believed to have direct contact with the gods. Some held the conviction that the bee was a manifestation of the soul, once it had left the body. Therefore, the bee had to be told that the body to which it belonged was no longer alive, so the soul could go and live in peace and happiness. In medieval France, many believed that if a man dreamed of encountering a swarm of bees, he would soon lose his job.

Mr. Soren's nightmares continue, so he calls his friend Melissa. The two sit face-to-face at the dining room table, sipping wine and eating beef tenderloin with acorn squash.

"Why do you bother to teach these kids, if all they do is give you grief?" says Melissa, a music teacher at the high school. "It's not as if you need the money. Quit teaching and focus on your playing. The residents at Prairie Grove look forward to your visits."

Mr. Soren fingers the filigree on the handle of his teacup. "Without my piano students, I'd be surrounded by old people."

Melissa chuckles. "You've been old all your life."

Both the same age, John Soren and Melissa Fletcher had gone to the same music college a few miles out of town, he focusing on piano and she on violin. They met by accident, a situation that centered on the fact that each, unbeknownst to the other, was dating the same guy. When they found out, they terminated their respective relationships and have been friends ever since. He's seen her through the passing of her father and a kitchen fire, and she's seen him through the death of Aunt Melody and a tax audit. Both are committed to being single.

"Lord knows I'm no example with my passion for antique quilts," says Melissa, "but sometimes you need to look forward, especially now that you're alone."

Mr. Soren folds his arms. "And how am I going to do that?"

"Get out of the house. Go meet people."

"In this town?" says Mr. Soren, letting out a guffaw. "You must be kidding."

"Hey, why don't you go on one of those Costa Rica yoga retreats?"

"And have nothing to say, while everybody else mingles and has a good time? I think not. You have to be popular for that sort of thing."

Melissa reminds Mr. Soren of the people's choice awards he has received for teaching piano: "two years in a row."

"I'm popular because I'm cheap," says Mr. Soren.

The friends look at each other and burst out laughing.

"I didn't mean it *that* way," says Mr. Soren.

"First time I heard you laugh since Melody passed."

Recalling the circumstances surrounding his aunt's death, Mr. Soren places his right hand across his chest. Some time during Carol Morris's piano lesson, Melody Plebbete collapsed with a fatal heart attack in the parlor. Not until a few minutes after James had left—nearly two hours later—did Mr. Soren find his aunt, lying face up on the gold candytuft sofa, her white hair undone and dangling over the cherry-wood base. On the coffee table before her was a cup of tea, half drunk, and a few crumbs left over from the scone she had eaten. On the corner of her lip was a dab of honey. Tea, honey, and scones at 2 o'clock: That was her ritual. Something, either a fly or a bee, buzzed around the dead woman's open mouth.

"Maybe I do need a change of scenery," says Mr. Soren.

"Hallelujah," says Melissa.

After clearing the table, the two friends go searching on Facebook for old acquaintances. It's either that or listening to conservatory students perform on YouTube, and then providing detailed assessments of their playing. That's what Melissa and Mr. Soren do, when they get together. On Facebook Mr. Soren comes across a former flutist, who used to wear hot pants and smoke weed in the woods at the edge of campus. Now she's a hundred pounds heavier and living downstate. In her spare time, she's a deaconess at some mega church with a mission "to preserve the American family by defining marriage as a sacred union between a man and a woman." When the two friends search the site for the church, they learn that a former parishioner is suing the minister for using "vomit therapy" to "cure" her son of homosexuality. Melissa comes across a newspaper article on the lawsuit.

"Take a look at the lawyer representing the mother and her poor kid," says Melissa. "Not bad. Can't be more than 60."

Mr. Soren studies the photo accompanying the article. The lawyer is small-boned and well-dressed, a face with creases and furrows in all the right places, indentations and lines that tell the story of a man in touch with his feelings. "I feel like I've seen this guy somewhere before."

"Didn't you used to know somebody by the name of Francis Trent?" asks Melissa.

Mr. Soren grabs the mouse and highlights the name below the picture. "That's the boy who gave me flowers, back when we were children."

* * *

The day of James's next lesson, the temperatures take a dip. Since Mr. Soren's already small bladder seems to shrink in the cold, he consumes less water, but to no avail. Right in the middle of fixing James's fingering for the lullaby, he excuses himself to go to the bathroom.

"Practice," says Mr. Soren, nearly running into the credenza as he looks back at the boy.

When he returns, the piano bench is empty.

"James, where are you?"

No one answers.

Scanning the room, Mr. Soren notices the sliding mahogany door to the parlor slightly ajar. He pushes it open. When he enters the room, the piano teacher stops abruptly. Lying face up, nude, on the gold candytuft sofa, James hums *The Cradle Song*. His hair dangles over the cherry-wood base, as he reaches into the air, going over the fingering Mr. Soren has taught him. James's body is smooth and opaque, the exposed armpits reminding the teacher of a matching set of ancient cremation urns he and his aunt had seen at a museum. Mr. Soren opens his mouth to speak, but nothing comes out, except a string of drool he immediately catches with his fingers.

"Are you gay?" says James, suddenly sitting up.

The boy's words send signals to the man's sciatic nerve. Mr. Soren begins to feel pressure in his stomach and chest. He imagines his torso filled with bees. He places his hands on the back of the sofa to keep from falling. The boy stands.

"Now just pretend, for a moment, that I'm a worker bee," says James, his voice cracking. "Now watch me do the waggle dance."

James wiggles his buttocks while forming a figure eight between the sofa and credenza, his fingers playing imaginary notes in the air. On the third cycle, he begins to chant. "Here, little bees, I've got some news. Now follow my fingering, so you can feed the nectar to the queen."

Mr. Soren flinches. "Put . . . on . . . your clothes," he says, his voice crescendoing with each successive word.

James obeys. Mr. Soren tells him to leave.

In the middle of the porch steps, the boy turns around. "I saw you," he says, two parallel lines forming between his eyebrows as he speaks. "I saw you in the back yard. You did your naked dance. Why can't I do mine? And how come, when I finally practice, you assign me a baby song?"

"I didn't . . ."

James interrupts: "I am practically an adult!"

As the boy goes running down the block, Mr. Soren gently shuts the door. He returns to the music room and fetches his old diary. When he opens it, bits of dried goldenrod, brown and brittle, drop to the floor. He takes the book into the parlor and sits down on the sofa. Turning the pages, he tries to remember how he had felt, when Aunt Melody had taken him out of school, when he was 14. He opens to an entry entitled Francis Trent and reads: "Why did he give me flowers? My chest feels funny, like something's happening inside. The feeling is both good and bad. It scares me, but I don't want it to go away. Why does Aunt Melody forbid me to talk about Francis Trent? I like him."

Mr. Soren puts down the diary and lies down on the candytuft couch. He closes his eyes and inhales, taking in the scent of James's body—sour feet, sugared sweat—the smell of a 14-year-old boy, his own smell, when *he* was that age. Johnny Plebbete had refused to wear socks. His aunt used to spray his shoes with disinfectant, "to keep down the stench," she had said. For breakfast Johnny ate sugared cereal, and if it had been up to him, candy bars would have sufficed for both lunch and dinner. He was grounded for a month, after telling his aunt's best friend that her voice sounded like a cat coughing up a fur ball in the key of e-flat. Mr. Soren examines his hands—too small for Rachmaninoff, splotched with age spots. He feels his breath tickle the tip of his nose and settles into slumber. He dreams he is lying right where he is, reading a science fiction novel. The story focuses on a society in which carefully selected adults are required by law to show adolescents how to handle their hormones. Parents, teachers, and other community leaders must disrobe and perform a dance that emulates the behavior of bees. When Mr. Soren awakens, he calls Melissa, recounts the incident with James.

"What do you think I should do?" he asks.

"Nothing," says Melissa. "Let it pass."

Mr. Soren heads out the front door to examine the hedge. The garden and fountain are hidden by seven feet of Hatfield yews. Imagining James climbing to the top for a peek, Mr. Soren grabs onto the hedge. It bends easily in his hands. On the ground he finds a blue button, picks it up, and goes into the house.

Before going to bed, Mr. Soren sends the following email to James's parents:

Dear Mr. and Mrs. Plimpton:
I am sorry to inform you that I will no longer be able to give piano

lessons to your son James. Things are simply not working out. I will be happy to make suggestions for another teacher, if you like.
Sincerely,
Mr. John Soren

Mr. Soren takes a sleeping pill and goes to bed. The next morning he calls to make an appointment to see Francis Trent for legal advice about the incident with James but hangs up before anyone answers. While he is having his tea and poached egg on toast, the doorbell rings. A tall, thick-boned woman wearing a navy-blue power suit steps forward.

"I'm Elaine Plimpton," says the woman, "James's mother."

Mr. Soren stands still. He has only met James's father, who had accompanied the boy for his first piano lesson. James looks like his father—small-boned and petite. The Plimptons live only a few blocks away.

For a moment, Mr. Soren contemplates slamming the door. Instead, he opens it wider and invites Mrs. Plimpton inside. They sit on the candytuft sofa.

"May I offer you some tea?" says Mr. Soren, his voice muddy and weak.

Before Mrs. Plimpton can answer, her cell phone rings, and she excuses herself to talk. As he waits, Mr. Soren envisions James's mother accusing him of molesting her son. He feels his breath shorten and takes a deep inhalation. As he exhales, he finds himself back in middle school, leafing through his French-English dictionary, while Madame Millous prattles on about the conjugation of *prendre,* the infinitive of the verb *take.* Buried in the *p*'s is *pédé,* a slang word for a gay man. Not until he went to college did he learn the linguistic relationship between *pédé* and pedophilia. Between that discovery and the fear of disease, he never pursued anyone. The man he had unknowingly shared with Melissa had gone after *him,* not vice versa. The so-called relationship lasted a month—30 days of intimate human contact out of 60 years of life.

Mr. Soren looks at the woman before him—confident, professional—talking to a client. Most importantly, she is socially adept, at least in the modern sense. Melody Plebbete would find the woman's behavior both rude and unacceptable, but after all, his aunt lived in another time—still wore gloves to drive and refused to speak to anyone who cursed. Mrs. Plimpton instructs the person on the other line—a man with a loud voice—how to install software onto his computer: "Click on" this, "drop down" to that. Her words are clear and specific. When the man loses patience and raises his voice, she talks him through his problem, keeping her cool. Mr. Soren is no match for Mrs. Plimpton—too smart to resort to violence, savvy enough to get him locked up for good. Flash a baby picture of her only son from her fancy iPhone, and a jury would melt. Some smart lawyer would find out that Mr. Soren practices yoga and modern dance in the nude. His diary would be on exhibit—proof in writing that he liked a boy. His picture would be plastered on the front page of the local newspaper. He'd be the top story on *Eyewitness News at Ten*. In prison, the inmates would take no time to rape and kill him. His house would go to the state. Perhaps the mega church would buy it, turn it into a new fellowship hall, preach against Mr. Soren and "sinful" people like him. No one would tell the bees when Mr. Soren dies.

"Mr. Soren," says Mrs. Plimpton, her thumbs going wild as she performs some complicated fingering on her phone after hanging up, "I came to ask why you suddenly decided to stop teaching my son. You didn't give a reason in your email. Did something happen? James won't say a thing."

Mr. Soren looks at her blankly. He can think of nothing to say—nothing that she or anyone else would ever accept. In a world without judgment, this conversation would not be happening. John Soren would be another person. Instead of panicking, he would have told the boy to dress. He would have asked him why he had chosen his piano teacher for such a demonstration. He would have been comfortable enough with his own sexuality to talk freely. He would have realized that James was too busy discovering himself to worry about convention—stuck in that in-between stage—a boy at play with his changing body, something Johnny Plebbete almost never did. Instead of turning him away, Mr. Soren could have shown him the diary, the pieces of goldenrod that Francis Trent had given him, once upon a time, before it was too late.

Mrs. Plimpton folds her arms. "Did James take off his clothes in front of you, shake his butt, and run around the room?"

Mr. Soren's jaw drops.

"I thought so," says Mrs. Plimpton. "He's been doing that a lot lately. 'Feeling his oats,' my mother-in-law said, when he did it to her. I call him 'the dancing bee.' "

Shivers run through Mr. Soren's body—the same feeling he had had at Melissa's, after he helped put out the fire.

Mrs. Plimpton apologizes for her son's behavior at Mr. Soren's house. "James makes up for his precociousness—you know he skipped two grades—by behaving childishly," she says. "We don't punish him. The kids at school give him a hard enough time."

"Why is that?" asks Mr. Soren, his voice barely a whisper.

"Around other kids, he's quiet, different, not well-liked. If it weren't for his older brother, who's in the same class and makes sure no harm comes to him, we'd have to resort to homeschooling."

Mr. Soren lets out a sigh. "I see."

Mrs. Plimpton slaps her hands against her lap. "If I get James to promise never to take off his clothes or perform his dancing bee act ever again in your presence, will you take him back? He really likes you, and I want you to be his teacher, that is, if you're willing."

Mr. Soren studies Mrs. Plimpton's face. Certainly she knows that James has little interest in the piano. "Don't you think he would be happier doing something outside—something other than sitting with an old man trying to play an instrument? Perhaps he could join the boy scouts."

Mrs. Plimpton stands up. "My 14-year-old son is gay. He has no role models, no one except for his piano teacher, and you're suggesting he join the Boy Scouts!"

"I didn't know."

Mrs. Plimpton apologizes for her outburst and sits down. She gazes at the hardwood floor, her lips crimped tightly, as if she wants to say something but refuses to let it out.

A trickle of sweat runs down the side of Mr. Soren's face.

"Considering we've never met," he says, "you seem to know a great deal about me."

Mrs. Plimpton raises her eyes. "Peter Ellis is my uncle—the guy you dated in college."

Mr. Soren puts his hands on his forehead. He remembers the passion he had shared with the one person he had allowed himself to touch, the one man he had allowed to touch him. And that was Mrs. Plimpton's uncle. So many years later, and the memory feels unimportant, as if it were a natural part of growing up, except he, John Soren, had never moved on, had never gotten over the fear of being himself. Even if he had failed to discover that Peter Ellis was dating Melissa Fletcher, he knew that his month-long affair was just that. He never really cared for Peter. Yet he had been so wrapped up with concealing his sexuality that such a realization was buried as well. Knowing that Peter meant little to him gives Mr. Soren a sense of satisfaction. He removes his hand from his forehead and places it on his lap.

"So, what is Peter up to these days?" asks Mr. Soren.

"Lives in Chicago," says Mrs. Plimpton. "Owns a bed and breakfast. Do you want me to put you in touch with him?"

"No."

"Well, then what about my son?" says Mrs. Plimpton, her tone neither angry nor pleasant. "Are you going to take him back or not?"

Mr. Soren is at a loss for words. He had never imagined that the outcome of his conversation with James's mother would depend on *his* decision and not hers. He, a role model: such a notion seems absurd, yet the prospect gives him energy. He can feel it in his chest—a space opening up. It's as if he has been given a code, a way to find happiness, but from the most unlikely source: James, the worker bee performing the waggle dance. At the age of 60, Mr. Soren will have to look elsewhere—beyond Melissa, his students, the people at Prairie Grove—to fill that space. He imagines a framed picture of himself holding another man, placed on top of the credenza for all to see. But what would he say, when Carol Morris or her mother asks, "Who is that, your brother?" Mr. Soren has no idea how he would respond. In order to be a proper role model, he'll need to get one for himself.

∞

Mr. Soren agrees to keep James as a student. Mrs. Plimpton tilts her head and smiles. She accepts the cup of tea Mr. Soren had offered earlier and admires the gold filigree on the handle. Then the piano teacher offers a plate of scones with honey. They eat, drink, and talk about the nice weather—a good day to be outside enjoying the fall wildflowers, Mrs. Plimpton says. Weather like this won't last, Mr. Soren adds. When James's mother leaves, Mr. Soren puts on his best suit and fetches a bouquet of goldenrods from the field beyond the garden.

Tinker Bell Laundry Detergent

Warnings and Disclaimers

Use Tinker Bell Laundry Detergent at your own risk. Whatever happens is the sole responsibility of the user. Of no relation to the fairy for whom the detergent is named, the employees of N8chur-Maid Products, or the writer of this story, I, your narrator, neither support nor oppose the promotion and/or sale of the product. Furthermore, I refuse to take responsibility for any mishaps or unusual behavior that may be linked with using the detergent or reading beyond this paragraph. I will, however, provide you with the following warning: Do not attempt to perform Tinker Bell's dances. They are the sole property of the fairy, who will come after you, if, in any way, you try to reproduce even the slightest bit of choreography described in this true account, which has been approved by Tink herself. It is best if readers believe or at least pretend to believe in fairies. Good luck and remember to use the gentle cycle when washing your imagination after reading this story.

Radio Commercial

If you're anything like me, you don't give a flying fairy about commercials and have little interest in laundry detergent. And once you hear the deep, exaggerated macho-male voice advertising Tinker Bell Laundry Detergent, you'll probably roll your eyes, just like I did when I first heard the following commercial on WXYZ FM Radio 91.3:

Remember how Tinker Bell drank poison to save Peter Pan? Yep, she survived, thanks to those that believed. And now, as long as you believe, the fairy with the fancy wings is here to help. All you have to do is sprinkle lightly on soiled garments, and Tinker Bell Laundry Detergent, fortified with Fairy Dust, will eliminate millions of poisons lurking deep in the fabric of your clothes: mold, mildew, bacteria, and smells that normal detergents can't even come close to fighting. Once you start using Tinker Bell, you'll be dancing with the stars, as those nasty stains and odors fly away to Never Neverland. Tinker

Bell Laundry Detergent: Natural, Hypoallergenic, and Fairy Flower scents. Both in liquid and powder form. Good for the environment. For inquiries and tips about how to save the planet while having fun with Tinker Bell Products, you can reach us online at www.tinkerbell.com/ neverland or call us at 777-TINKERBELL.

Stats
- Wonderfully large for a fairy, Tinker Bell spans the length of Rachmaninoff's right hand, from pinkie to thumb, stretching from C to A.
- However, you mustn't look for Tink because you won't see her. Very few do, and you probably aren't willing to go through the sacrifices required to catch no more than a glimpse. The closest you'll get is a solid bronze likeness.
- The Great Ormond Street Hospital for Children in London sports a statue of the fairy: fit and graceful, with the high arches of a ballerina, as well as two sets of wings—one for flying and the other for sprinkling Fairy Dust on both friends and foes.

Tinker Bell's Director
Throughout most of this story, Tinker Bell works for Fey Queen, the 35-year-old human CEO of N8chur-Maid Products, the parent company for Tinker Bell Laundry Detergent, Stay Healthy Blueberry Products, and Boreal Food Supplements. A former professional dancer with the Martha Graham Dance Company, Queen lives alone in a million-dollar tree house and spends her free time practicing pagan celibacy. Before she changed her name for the stage, Fey Queen used to be Gretchen Schlump.

The Relationship between Fey Queen and Tinker Bell
Queen first came into contact with Tinker Bell while on tour in Montreal. Under eating, as some dancers do to maintain an ideal weight, the future CEO failed to consume enough calories after a sold-out show. On her day off, the dancer took a walk up Mount Royal and passed out, landing on a soft bed of mushrooms. Tinker Bell, a lover of modern dance, found the dancer, granted her the right to see fairies, and fed her blueberries, nursing her back to health in time for the next day's performance. Queen

91

danced exquisitely, and a friendship was struck between the dancer and the fairy. When the dancer sustained a serious ankle injury several years later, Tinker Bell gave up her bell to save Queen from becoming permanently disabled. When Queen recovered, she taught the fairy and her colleagues to dance. With the support of Tink, Queen went back to school to study communications and business administration. No longer in possession of a special bell, Tinker Bell now speaks through dance. Wearing the bell on her pierced belly button, Fey Queen is the only adult, with the exception of a few gay men, granted the power to see fairies. Most children can see them naturally.

Tinker Bell's Former Place of Residence

Before things went wrong, Tinker Bell and her fairy colleagues lived a few miles from Queen in the crook of an oak, at the junction of the pluperfect tense and the *Avenue de Ciel Bleu*. This northern region had traditionally remained off limits to fairies because of religious intolerance. However, Tinker Bell moved there to be close to her friend and to help humans who had become emotionally, intellectually, and spiritually underprivileged because of corporate greed and technological mayhem. Unlike people, fairies produce a minimal impact on the environment and are quite conservative in terms of their depletion of natural resources. As dancers with feet as light as meringue, the fairies living on the *Avenue* easily refrained from trampling the rhizomes that enable indigenous lowbush blueberries to spread. It is here that Tinker Bell came up with an idea to put Fairy Dust in laundry detergent.

How Fairy Dust Works

Ever since the first fairies were born, they have produced Fairy Dust. While fluttering at high speeds, their diaphanous wings secrete creative antioxidants, which take the shape of a chain. Between the links of the chain lie a variety of posthypnotic suggestions produced by the fairies. Once the dust falls on a human being, the suggestions become absorbed. Unfortunately, some suggestions lose their potency because of ozone depletion. But thanks to the low-bush wild blueberries located in the region surrounding the *Avenue de Ciel Bleu,* Fairy Dust has regained some of its strength. When Tinker Bell choreographed a fluttering dance, the dust's potency increased tremendously. When producing Fairy Dust for Tinker Bell Laundry Detergent, Tink and her corps of fairies flutter danced over large vats of swirling soap to produce a most unusual and effective product.

Subversion of Rule

According to author J. M. Barrie, Tinker Bell was either all good or all bad because fairies are so small they can only have one feeling at a time. This was true when Barrie wrote *Peter and Wendy,* the story most people know as *Peter Pan.* However, since the time of publication, Tinker Bell has grown and evolved to support multiple feelings at a single moment. Such growth has been achieved mainly through Tink's experiences with children, Peter and Wendy beginning a series of relationships that have gone unnoticed by the adult world, with the exception of Fey Queen. Thanks to internet technology, Tink and other fairies can upload a variety of feelings onto a cloud. Finally, when they perform their dances and consume vast quantities of wild blueberries, eloquent, socially motivated movement interacts with antioxidants to support character development.

Tinker Bell's Persona

Created by the imagination of Barrie, Tinker Bell is both a fairy and a child advocate. In her spare time, she focuses a great deal of attention on supporting sick, injured, disabled, and abused children. Originally a tinker, meaning someone who fixes pots and pans, Tinker Bell has seen firsthand the dire results of childhood accidents, particularly in the kitchen. A mere scratch, she has determined, can be avoided with proper precaution, instruction, and habits. Tinker Bell's dedication to children stands unprecedented. In some cases, she monitors parents to make sure that children are being treated properly. For example, in the case of Estuary, a precocious 7-year-old, Tink arranged for his verbally abusive father to land a job that keeps him traveling for much of the year. The fairy can't stand to see a child being humiliated and will go to extreme lengths to see that such behavior is stopped. It's important to note that Tinker Bell suffers from a bit of a temper.

Tinker Bell's Dances

Think butterfly meets Martha Graham. If Tinker Bell allowed eminent critics to view her work, the fairy's choreography might be described as having the lyrical yet succinct earthiness of the Graham technique, alongside the gossamer ethereality of a monarch riding a breeze. Although her repertoire goes unrivaled in terms of its vast scope and variety of styles, all of Tinker Bell's dances flout convention. Hence every box or bottle of Tinker Bell Laundry Detergent produced by the fairy and her corps of dancers is unique, since different movements and moods produce different types of Fairy Dust. Unbeknownst to the FDA, Tink makes sure that testing is done on only the most innocuous batches of product. What the public purchases is not so neutral. For example, Tinker Bell and company perform an extremely lyrical and long-winded healing dance for all batches that go to children's hospitals.

A Live Appearance, Part I

Quite dedicated to her charity work, Tinker Bell makes live appearances at homes, hospitals, and schools, visiting a variety of places to see how children are getting along. Such was the case this past summer at a daycare center sandwiched in a shopping center, between a Michael's and a Best Buy.

Now I'd like you to stop reading and come with me to see Tinker Bell make one of her most noteworthy appearances. How long will it take? Not long, if you fly. Just like Peter and Wendy, let's "think lovely wonderful thoughts," so "they can lift [us] up in the air." Close your eyes and follow me: "Second to the right and straight on till morning." Oh, I almost forgot. You can't fly without a sprinkling of Fairy Dust. Poof! That should be enough.

Welcome. It's nice to go back in time, especially when you get to be a kid again. Why don't you put yourself over there on the floor, between the children and the kitchen. Careful— you're invisible. If somebody stands up, get out of the way. That's Estuary's mother Maureen on your right, reading *Peter Pan* to the kids. She owns the place. No, your imagination is not working overtime. I hear the same crashes and screams that you do. Somebody's playing a video game at Best Buy. But Maureen seems to be managing quite well, even though her helper didn't show up for work. Quite a woman with her booming, expressive voice. You can tell how she loves to read to the kids. Now, as you listen, I want you to watch for Tinker Bell. She's about to make her entrance. "You see, Wendy," reads Maureen, "when the first baby laughed for the first time, its laugh broke into a thousand pieces, and they all went skipping about, and that was the beginning of fairies." Look! There she is: Tinker Bell dancing to the story. No, Maureen cannot see her; as much as she loves *Peter Pan*, she is an adult who doesn't believe in fairies. Just listen to those kids squeal with delight, as their graceful hero flutters and swoops. I love this part, when Maureen laughs with them. Just ignore the sounds from the store, and it feels like you're inside a Currier and Ives print of the twenty-first century. Makes you want to join in. Feels good; doesn't it?

A Live Appearance, Part II

Well, I'm sorry to spoil the fun, but I want you to focus your attention on Estuary, the 7-year-old boy with the curly brown hair. No, he's not in the circle. Look in the kitchen area—to your right, where baby Twyla is lying in her crib. Penelope Fenster, Twyla's mother and Maureen's best friend since childhood, has asked the daycare center owner to mind her baby during the workday, until she can raise enough money for a nanny. Maureen has agreed wholeheartedly, especially since Twyla is so well-behaved. See Twyla's crib, the boy softly tiptoeing up to it? I know; you can't tell what's going on. Neither can Tink. But look out! Here she comes with her obligatory kitchen flyover, to make sure that the children and pots and pans are all in order. What's she doing? Dancing and sprinkling Fairy Dust all over the boy. It's hard to see in that big cloud of dust. Oh, no. It can't be. Blood dripping from the boy's arms. You can almost hear baby Twyla whimpering in her crib. What happened? Quick! Come back to the present, and I'll tell you.

What the Boy Does

Quite the opposite of his robust mother sitting on her armchair reading *Peter Pan*, undersized Estuary sneaks away from the circle, as the children laugh and marvel over Tinker Bell's dance. Imagining that her dramatic reading has inspired the children to delight, Maureen revels in her moment of perceived fame, failing to see her son tiptoeing toward Twyla's crib. Even if she did see him, she wouldn't think much, for he has always been a sweet boy. Through the plastic bars, he feeds the charger cord of his mother's iPhone, so it dangles just above Twyla's fingers. Allowing her to play with the cord, he leans like a mannequin, seemingly suspended in space and time. A minute passes. The baby plays contentedly. Estuary unfastens the top three buttons of the tiny dress Twyla's mother had designed and sewed. Then, slowly and deliberately with the metal piece that fits into the phone, he scratches the baby's belly, lightly at first, and then more intensely. With his sharp instrument, he draws a triangle with a line running through it. A preemie who has endured the pain of open-chest surgery, Twyla fails to cry. Instead, she shakes while letting out a few inaudible whimpers.

The Dance that Stops the Boy

Through the synchronistic movement of her wings, spine, and breath, Tinker Bell hovers over Estuary, performing a series of Martha Graham contractions, each successively faster and more forceful, like waves tumbling onto the beach during a gale. Blueberry juice, a prime ingredient in Tink's sweat, coupled with Fairy Dust from the pores in her wings, interacts with remnants of Tinker Bell Laundry Detergent on Estuary's clothes. Such a potent concoction, alongside the fairy's intention expressed through the art of modern dance, causes the boy to break out in hives. Immediately, he stops scratching Twyla and uses the phone cord to gouge himself bloody. Almost flying into Maureen's nose she's so upset, Tinker Bell escapes the daycare center.

What Happens after Tinker Bell Leaves

Penelope arrives to pick up her baby. "Don't ask because I don't know," blurts Maureen, as she wraps her son's arms in Ace bandages. "This is a nightmare." Penelope puts her arm around her friend. "What can I do?" Maureen shakes her head, and Penelope turns to Estuary, now sitting on his mother's lap.

"How did you get those terrible scratches?" she asks the boy. "I had an itch," says Estuary, as if his bloody arms are no big deal. "The hurt will go away," says Maureen, her legs beginning to shake. Estuary claims his arms don't hurt. Penelope dials 911 on her cell, but quickly hangs up because Twyla starts to cry. Penelope runs to her daughter's crib. "I know, baby," she says, stroking the blond curls drooping across Twyla's forehead. "The grownups are all upset, and so are you." Penelope checks the baby's diaper—clean and dry. Then she feels her forehead— slightly warm. As the other parents arrive, Maureen takes Estuary to the bathroom. With Twyla in her arms, still crying, Penelope straightens the room. "Where's Maureen?" says Kate, whose son Ken gets picked on by the other boys for being quiet and polite. "Estuary's had an accident," says Penelope. "As soon as the parents leave, we're going to the ER." Kate offers to help, and Penelope refuses politely. On his way out, Ken asks if Twyla is OK. "She's just upset about Estuary," says Penelope, turning to her daughter. "That's right. You're a sensitive little girl. And when your friend gets hurt, you feel bad."

At the ER

Estuary is treated for his scratches, which are now infected. Twyla, whose crying intensifies, is examined and treated for her scratches, which are prominent but not infected. The ER intern, a heavyweight with yellow teeth and smoker's breath, snarls at Penelope: "Why did you fail to report the scratches on your baby's stomach?" "I didn't see them," says Penelope, now in tears. "She was wearing a dress, and I didn't look underneath, not even when I felt her diaper. I didn't think to. I'm sorry." The ER intern files two reports—one for Estuary and the other for Twyla—of possible abuse. The baby and the boy are transferred to the children's unit of the hospital for further observation. Both mothers arrange to stay overnight.

Estuary's Interview with a Caseworker

A baby-faced woman with a haircut similar to that of Mary Martin in the 1960 TV movie *Peter Pan* interviews Estuary. "Did someone hurt you?" says the caseworker. "No," says Estuary. The caseworker places her hand on Estuary's shoulder and tells him it's all right to tell the truth. "You won't be tattling, if you tell me who it was." Estuary shakes his head. "It was no one." The caseworker asks Estuary to tell him what happened. "A rat bit me," he says. "Did someone tell you to tell me that?" asks the caseworker. "No," says Estuary. The caseworker asks the boy what he wants to be when he grows up. "An artist," he says, "but don't tell anyone, especially my father."

Estuary and Twyla

Whenever Penelope brought Twyla over to the house, he loved to hold, feed, and rock the baby to sleep. Both his mother and her friend knew his interest was pure and full of grace. But Hank, his father, thought otherwise and told him he looked like "a girl with her prissy doll baby." This was when Tinker Bell sprinkled Fairy Dust on Hank's supervisor, who ended up promoting Hank to international sales. Later, some of the boys at school called Estuary bad names for being nice to girls. When summer came, and he had to hang out with his mother at daycare, one boy told him he might turn into a baby girl, if he spent too much time playing with Twyla. He told his mother what the boy said, and she advised him to ignore the remarks. One day, after watching a violent TV show, Estuary came up with the idea of hurting the baby—just a little—in order to prove he was a boy. Excuse me a moment, while I smash up a few televisions and satellites.

Penelope and the Caseworker

The baby-faced caseworker insists on interviewing Penelope at her home, a partially restored green and pink Victorian in the historic district. Since the parlor is under construction, the contractor's tools scattered across the floor, the women sit in the kitchen at an old Formica table. "Why such a big house for two people?" asks the caseworker. Penelope explains that her husband died last year, just as they had embarked on a project to turn their home into a bed and breakfast. The caseworker scribbles something into her electronic notebook. "Do you let your daughter play in the living room?" she asks. "Of course not," says Penelope, immediately sorry for her defensive tone, yet offended by the caseworker, whom she imagines as a formerly abused child, suspicious of all parents. The unwanted visitor asks Penelope why she didn't report her daughter's injuries, and Penelope slowly repeats her explanation about not knowing. The caseworker asks why not. Penelope looks her in the eye: "I am not accustomed to undressing my child every time she cries. There are ways of checking if a baby is wet or soiled, without taking off every item of clothing. My baby was dry. She's never even had diaper rash. Since the blood from the scratches did not seep through her clothing, I saw nothing. I love my daughter dearly and can't imagine abusing a child. Even the idea of it horrifies me." Fighting back tears, Penelope clears her throat, then apologizes for her frustrated tone. The caseworker asks if she has ever seen a therapist. The answer is no. "Are you involved in any community organizations, such as clubs or churches?" Penelope tells her there's no time because of her commitment to raising Twyla, working, and overseeing the renovations. "Do you have any hobbies?" Penelope remembers the wonderful modern dance performance that Maureen and she had attended last year, not long before her husband's fatal heart attack. "No," she says. "No hobbies and no boyfriends, in case you want to know."

The Caseworker's Meeting with Maureen

Maureen forces herself to appear calm, as she answers all questions about parenting, the daycare center, and her friendship with Penelope. When the caseworker asks about Maureen's husband, she refers to him as traditional and strict. Although they have grown apart as a result of his poor attitude and old-fashioned ideas, she takes care not to say anything negative about the man she is supposed to love. "Could your husband have injured Estuary and Twyla?" asks the caseworker, ignoring Maureen's statement that Hank has been overseas for two weeks. "No," says Maureen. "That's impossible." The caseworker asks what baby Twyla was doing at the daycare center in the first place. "I was doing a favor for a friend," says Maureen.

Estuary and Maureen

A nurse assures Maureen that Estuary's scratches are not rat bites. When his infection subsides, he is released into her custody. Maureen takes him back to the daycare center, which she has decided to close for a week. She asks him to remember what happened. Dragging his feet, he begins to open and shut cabinets. "Why did you name me Estuary?" he asks his mother. "Dad said you were on drugs." Maureen shakes her head and puts her arms on her son's shoulders. "You hurt Twyla on purpose, didn't you?" she says. "Why would you do such a thing?" Mother and son stare into each other's eyes. A minute passes. Estuary hands his mother a half-empty box of Tinker Bell Laundry Detergent, featuring a fairy performing a lunge in midair. "Were you fooling around with this the day that Twyla was hurt?" his mother asks. The boy nods his head. "The only time I ever got my way with your father was when I named you. I've read to you about estuaries—protectors of plants and animals. Your birth was my protection."

Twyla and Penelope

Twyla is kept in the children's unit for further observation. Tinker Bell makes a visit. When the scabs on Twyla's scratches develop bright apple-red sparkles, the doctors don't know what to think. Penelope makes sure to keep close to her daughter. She looks into the golden-brown irises of Twyla's eyes and tries to discern the truth. "Who hurt you?" she whispers. "Was it Estuary? Did he do this to you?" Raised in a Quaker household, Penelope does not believe in violence. It's getting more difficult to keep from blaming her best friend and her best friend's son, for her daughter's injuries.

Tinker Bell's Meeting with Fey Queen

Tinker Bell performs a dance of desperation for her employer. "You did your best," says Queen, who suggests that Tinker Bell seek the advice of Peter Pan, now living in New York with his husband. Both men practice child psychology.

Tinker Bell's Meeting with Peter Pan

"Visit Estuary," says Peter, his gray goatee bobbing up and down as he pronounces the boy's name. "Get him to tell his mother what really happened. If that doesn't work, go find the boy's father and convince him to talk to his son, get the child to open up." Tinker Bell rolls her eyes. Peter reminds her of Wendy's father, who redeemed himself at the end of the story. Tinker Bell performs a dance, one part bombastic and the other lyrical, to indicate that she sees little in common, with the exception of stupidity, between Hank and Wendy's father.

Tinker Bell's Visit with Estuary

Estuary and his parents live in a large ranch home built in the late '80s. His father still away, the boy is asleep in his bedroom. Tinker Bell waits. When Estuary awakens, he neither sees nor hears the fairy, not even when she performs a dance that recounts his abuse of Twyla. Disappointed and saddened by the child's inability to recognize fairies, Tinker Bell leaves.

Maureen and Penelope

Maureen meets with Penelope to figure out how to prepare for the preliminary hearing, in which a judge will either turn Twyla over to her mother or grant temporary custody to the state, while an in-depth investigation is conducted. Best friends since they shared the role of a fairy in dance class when they were both 12, the two never argue, and when they disagree, it's usually over who will pay for lunch. Now they sit in Penelope's kitchen, face to face. Letters of reference praising Penelope as a mother lay strewn on the table. Both women avoid eye contact. Maureen reveals a theory that Estuary gave Twyla Tinker Bell Laundry Detergent to play with. "They both must have had an allergic reaction to the detergent," says Maureen. "Don't you buy the hypoallergenic variety?" says Penelope, refraining from mentioning the unlikelihood of a baby scratching designs into her own stomach, allergic reaction or not. "The store was out of it." The women decide to borrow money and hire a private investigator to find out more about the product. If they can prove that the detergent is to blame for their children's injuries, they will sue N8chur-Maid Products.

Tinker Bell's Visit to Estuary's Father

Handsome and alluring in a rugged sort of way, Hank sells farm implements. His current project has brought him to northern Maine with a robotic arm designed to pick wild blueberries deep in the forest, where contemporary picking machines could never navigate. Presenting the arm at a special convention of organic food producers, Estuary's father is confident and amenable. Fey Queen is present. "With the robot picker, you'll not only get into those hard-to-reach places, but you'll also cut your costs in half," says Estuary's father. "I want to see the arm in action, and then I'd like a detailed report on how it works," says Queen. "Haven't I seen you somewhere before?" says Estuary's father. Tinker Bell breaks into the meeting, but the boss says she's busy. The fairy flees in defeat.

The Hearing and its Outcome

During Tinker Bell's flight back to Maureen and Penelope's hometown, the caseworker insists that Penelope's Victorian is unsafe for her daughter to live in. Photos of the renovations are produced, and temporary custody of Twyla is granted to the state, while a formal investigation is conducted. A local newspaper prints a story saying the state suspects a single mother of Satanic rituals, based on the triangle intersected by a line, on her baby's stomach. Estuary starts to tell his mother he was just drawing shapes, but stops when his father enters the room. Penelope receives harassing phone calls, hate mail, and death threats. The state shuts down Maureen's daycare center. The two best friends no longer speak to one another. Maureen pursues the lawsuit against Tinker Bell Laundry Detergent and N8chur-Maid Products, even though the investigator has yet to produce evidence against the company. Fey Queen fires Tinker Bell, gives up pagan celibacy, and proceeds to have an affair with Estuary's father. Penelope sells the Victorian to pay legal costs for her fight to keep Twyla.

Tinker Bell's Last-chance Dance

One by one, Tinker Bell visits the children from the daycare center, looking for someone who might have seen Estuary abuse Twyla. No matter how well the fairy dances the story, the children recollect nothing beyond her *Peter Pan* dance. She is down to the last child: Ken, who lives with his mother in a maximum-security condo with enough screens, gates, and locks to make Tink shake from fear that her wings will get caught. She barely makes it through the wire-mesh electric fence. Playing a game on his computer, Ken is happy to see the fairy, whose energy is at an all-time low, since she no longer has access to the world's most prolific wild blueberry bushes, which, unfortunately, are undergoing genetic modification in order to produce bigger berries that will better accommodate the robotic arm. "You look like you've been chased by the crocodile with the clock in its stomach," says Ken, referring to a scene from *Peter Pan*. Instead of performing a dance, Tinker Bell hops onto Ken's keyboard to punch in the YouTube url for Martha Graham's *Lamentation* solo: https://www.youtube.com/watch?v=xgf3xgbKYko

Another Break from Reading

So go ahead and take a look—it's only five minutes long—and see what you think. Of course the url works, unlike the one for Tinker Bell Laundry Detergent. I'll wait. Okay, so tell me: did the hair on your arms suddenly stand on end, when Graham talked about a woman from the audience, who witnessed her son getting run over by a truck? Not until she saw Graham's signature piece was the woman able to cry for the death of her son. Yep, you can argue that the sight of a solo dancer, dressed in a tube-like costume, cavorting in pain, is inappropriate for Ken or any 8-year-old boy. And perhaps you're right.

Return to Tink's Visit with Ken

After seeing the solo, Ken comes forward and tells what he had witnessed at the daycare center. When the judge asks him why he waited so long, he says he didn't want to be a tattletale. "You get called a girl, if you tattle."

What Happens after Ken Testifies

Maureen retracts her lawsuit against Tinker Bell Laundry Detergent and N8chur-Maid Products, after Twyla is released into the custody of her mother. Penelope and Maureen are still not talking. Estuary goes once a week to see a counselor. Despite Fey Queen's attempts to rehire Tinker Bell, the fairy ignores the CEO and heads to New York. Soon after, her fairy friends follow, refusing to work for someone they consider an abuser of power. Until she can find an unoccupied crook in an oak in Central Park, Tink stays with Peter and his husband. Her latest choreographic project is called The New York Strip. Tinker Bell, along with former N8chur-Maid fairies, has joined forces with a well-known maker of meat tenderizer to perform a dance that produces Fairy Juice—somewhat similar to Fairy Dust—which strips New York strip steaks of artery-clogging cholesterol. As a result of the fairies' occupation of New York, the city suffers from the mysterious loss of tens of gallons of blueberry juice from a variety of markets and stores. However, the production of Fairy Dust, which falls everywhere, has a profound effect: modern dance flash mobs take over Manhattan, and crime diminishes by 3 percent. When Tinker Bell is not working, she continues to visit hospitals, businesses, and homes; however, she no longer dances during story time.

New and Improved Tinker Bell Laundry Detergent

Maureen's ex-husband talks Fey Queen into using robots to produce genetically modified artificial Fairy Dust. Tinker Bell Laundry Detergent loses its potency. Yet the public continues to buy the product. In fact, sales increase significantly, despite the detergent's inability to fight dirt and save children. Queen has lowered the price by a dollar per container. After cutting the cost of production, she's doubled her profits. Consumers are happy, all except children and outliers, who turn to dance to make their lives worth living.

Come Dance with Me

Winter 1919

Grace accepts the job, says goodbye to her family, and sets sail on the Leviathan, bound for war-torn Turkey. On her first day at sea she starts a diary, in which she makes a vow to uphold her duties as a nurse for the American Committee for Relief in the Near East. For two years Grace has thwarted the affections of a surgeon attempting to shame her into a romance, claiming she would turn into an old maid, if she didn't settle soon. *I will not be forced into something I do not want,* Grace has said to the doctor many a time. She dips pen into ink. *The health and welfare of the Armenians in Turkey come first. If anyone ever gets his hands on this diary, let it be known that I am taking this position to help the unfortunate, not to find a husband.* Grace is 25, the surgeon, 42.

The exclamation point in the sentence fragment *Learning to speak Turkish!* contains a smudge caused by the movement of Grace's right hand, as the Leviathan pulls to starboard, somewhere in the Sargasso Sea. Her second diary entry is short, written in weak and wavy print, for Grace has discovered an innate inclination for seasickness: *I have fully decided never to take an ocean voyage just for pleasure, and to advise all family and friends to see America first.* Grace falls in and out of consciousness as the ship makes its way through precipitous swells and troughs. Dr. Bellson, easy to spot with his thick black handlebar mustache, cares for Grace. When the sea and her stomach return to a state of tranquility, Grace waltzes with Dr. Bellson during one of the ship's dances. *If ever I need an appendectomy, I trust the hands of Dr. Bellson,* writes Grace in the margins of her diary. *He moves me across the crowded dance floor as if he were slicing into flesh, cognizant of every layer of skin he penetrates, every organ he avoids.*

Fall 2014

Peter breaks up with Stephen, gets a checkup, and starts a diary. In the first entry, he makes a vow: *I decide how I spend my free time. Nobody else.* He signs the first letter of his first name in HIV negative blood and the rest in red ink. A professional actor, Stephen had called Peter boring in bed, just before the two broke up. *I need a change of pace,* writes Peter, before closing his diary and locking it in the secret drawer of his desk. Scrolling though the apps on his phone, he finds a meetup with the following description: *Travel the world without leaving town. Learn folk dances from six continents. Sounds possible,* says Peter, who loved to dance around the house when he was little. Unlike his father, a retired war correspondent for a major newspaper, Peter has no intention of ever leaving the country. Last month he turned 42. Stephen is 39. Both are in excellent shape.

The first *d* in the phrase *I did it!* contains a smudge caused by the dripping sweat of Peter's brow, deposited in his diary during a break at the International Folk Dancers' weekly meetup. His handwriting is a bit wavy, the steps of the last dance still reverberating through his body. *Judging by looks, I'm the youngest one in the group. We dance in a big room in the basement of the Unitarian Church. A heavy-set man with thin white suspenders taught the steps of an Armenian dance called the Kochari. We stand in a line interlinking pinkies. Then we swivel and jump and tip our bodies forward. The dance makes me feel different, like I'm learning to be someone else, but that person is also me. The teacher says the Kochari was designed to imitate the movement of sparring rams.* Peter switches from printing to cursive, red pen digging deeply into the beige lined page, as he imagines Stephen's disapproval of what he writes. *Nobody remotely attractive. Don't care. Last thing I need is sex. No condoms, no worries. Now I have dance.*

Winter 1972
Grace is finally well enough to spend time with the baby, her grandchild. *He's very particular,* warns Susan, Grace's daughter. In an attempt to bounce Peter very lightly on her knee, Grace experiences the shrillness of the baby's screams. At 78, her hearing is still in fine condition. *Doctor's report?* asks Grace. *Clean bill of health,* says Susan. Grace stands up, still holding the crying baby. *Let me try something,* she says. Twisting with a slight bow,

Grace imitates the movement of an Armenian mother trying to calm her baby during a siege of gunshot in the midst of a long-forgotten war. *We're dancing,* she sings. *Yes, we're dancing.* Peter stops crying and grabs his grandmother's pinkie.

Spring 1919

Grace and her colleagues arrive in Smyrna, Turkey. They move into abandoned boxcars in the freight yard, where they will remain until they can find a suitable home. Grace marvels at the stony hills and gorges. *A native gave us large bunches of lilacs. A pious Turk orders that a place be made on his tomb to catch water for birds. I saw a woman feeding an infant by first masticating the food and then putting it in the baby's mouth. There were donkeys leading camel chains. Men ride while women walk. These people need education, Christianity, and health centers with district nursing. I know I am here for a purpose.*

Winter 2014

Peter becomes a regular at the International Folk Dancers' weekly meetups. For the first half hour, a volunteer teaches new dances, and after that, the group moves from dance to dance without instruction. Peter works hard to commit some of the dances to memory. In addition to taking notes during class, he takes great care to record his impressions. *I couldn't believe it. Joe—got to be at least 60 and a fantastic dancer—gave me a red handkerchief. This means I was given the privilege of leading the Halay, Turkey's national dance. I love waving the hanky, stepping and bouncing, listening to the zurnas—so reedy, the music tickles a part of me I never knew existed. (Can just imagine the cracks Stephen would make, if he saw this entry.) Fran, Joe's wife, says I'm a natural folk dancer. Feel like I'm somewhere in Turkey—desert, rocks, camels. Dancing almost makes me want to go abroad.*

Spring 1993

A 60-year-old American journalist is killed during heavy gunfire between Muslim-led forces and Bosnian Croat soldiers in the city of Mostar. When the news comes across the TV, the journalist is not identified. Peter thinks his father is dead, until a phone call proves him wrong. Waiting with his mother at the airport, he runs his fingers across the embossed 21 on the birthday card his father had sent him from Europe. At the celebration dinner for his father's return, Peter orders a glass of wine, showing his identification to the waitress before she has a chance to ask. When the drink arrives, he hands it to his father, who asks him why he ordered it, if he didn't want it. *Just to see what it feels like to be 21,* he says. *You know I don't drink.* His mother lets out as guffaw, *Sometimes I wish you would,* she says. *Then you might learn to socialize with people your own age.* Peter's father praises his son for his individuality. His mother tells him that individuals sometimes end up alone. Peter's best friend is a 65-year-old woman, a docent at a local historic house open to the public during the warmer months. When they get together, they talk about antiques.

Spring 1919

Grace adjusts to her new surroundings. *I made hot biscuits for 14 of us. Then to the warehouse to help unload supplies. One of our hamals, a laborer trained from childhood to carry heavy loads on his back, tore the skin off his finger today, and to my surprise, he powdered it all over with tobacco from a cigarette and tied it up with a black rag. This to him was much better treatment than we would have given him.*

We borrowed the Victrola and had a little dance this evening. Dr. Bellson was in rare form. During the waltz, he counted one-two-three in English, Turkish, and Armenian. I started laughing as he spoke Armenian. When he uttered the word for two, his moustache bunched below his nose in such an odd yet adorable fashion that I couldn't help myself. Dr. Bellson is only 30.

Winter 2014

Peter reads on the internet about how the Turks *oppressed and then annihilated the Armenians in the early 1900s. Couldn't fall asleep. Thought about dancing the Turkish Halay. Joe's description of how to perform the steps made my arm hair stand on end. Give a little kick in the direction you're going, then a little kick in the direction you came from. Makes me think of an army invasion—death and destruction. Trying not to think negatively about Turks.*

Zoned out at work. Imagined I was dodging Turkish shrapnel. Strange thought: I wonder if folk dancing can keep people from warring. Act out frustrations through dance and avoid violence. Read somewhere that the Army prohibits soldiers from getting close to the culture of the people they're fighting. Went to dinner with Joe and Fran. He asked if I had a girlfriend, and she told him to mind his own business. I told them I'm gay. Seemed to go over well. Got a text from Stephen. Can't find his leather harness and wanted to know if I'd seen it. I said no.

Fall 1990

Two days after Peter's 18th birthday, his father accompanies him to the post office. Peter drives. On the way, Peter confesses that he hasn't the capacity to kill another human. His father says every American has the right to make such a decision. At the post office, Peter registers with Selective Service. On his way out, he looks into his father's hazel eyes and asks him if he would miss his job, if, suddenly, all wars ceased to exist. His father says, *No, definitely not.* On the way home, Peter's father asks him if he's sexually attracted to other young men. Peter stops the car on the side of the road. He says he's attracted to no one; he will never get AIDS, nor will he get a woman pregnant. His father assures him that he and his mother would support having a gay son. Peter says nothing.

Spring 1919

Grace receives the news at noon. *Smyrna was given to the Greeks. So now we are living in Greece! What rejoicing among the Greeks and what heartaches among the Turks and Armenians. At 1 p.m. word came that Dr. Bellson had taken over the whole Turkish hospital and wished me to come up. As we drove along, the people all cheered us, shouting, Americano! As our carriage came into view, both Greeks and Turks who were still shooting at each other across the street held their fire to let us pass, and then resumed their shooting. Armenians who had worn the Turkish fez for protection against*

109

discrimination were now going bare-headed.

A ship loaded with Armenian refugees stopped here today for six hours, and oh, the suffering I saw made me thank God for my blessings. Most of the people were in utter rags and so very dirty. Several of the girls had branded faces, done by the Arabs, and, in some cases, the marks were not yet healed. And the characteristic Arab indelible ink mark was to be found on many. Most of these women had husbands at one time, but the Turks had taken and killed them. Things are very tense and peace is to be signed in Paris tomorrow. What is to become of Smyrna no one knows.

Winter 2014

Peter receives a text from Joe and pulls out his diary. *Folk dancing is canceled tonight. Unitarian Church on same street as a fundamentalist Christian church. Christians planning a protest against proposed mosque a block away. Fundamentalists going to burn a page from the Koran on church grounds. Got a leaf-burning permit—means they can start fires with paper. Wish religions didn't exist. Text from Stephen. Invited me to a protest against the church and mosque. Texted Stephen and Joe with same message: got a stomachache, staying in.*

Don't know what's going on, but can hear gunshot, sirens, people shouting. Wish this room were soundproof. Vacuuming to drown out the noise. Stomach's gotten worse. Can't eat. Going to bed. Heard a huge bang and then felt like throwing up. Tried to but couldn't. Dry heaves. Just need to get through the night. Wish Stephen were here. Too busy dressing up in macho gay attire to worry about me. As if protesting in a leather harness is going to accomplish something amongst the fundamentalists and Muslims.

Winter 1973

At 79, Grace dies at home, a few hours after having an argument with her only daughter. Grace leaves her house to Susan and an annuity to Peter, to cover his college tuition. When her mother's house sells, Susan finds Grace's diary, chronicling her time in Turkey. Susan throws the diary in the trash, but then picks it up and puts it in a box, which ends up in the attic. Her husband finds the russet-colored volume with gold-leaf pages and places it on a bookshelf. No one reads the diary, and Susan eventually forgets about it.

Spring 1919

Grace deals with a difficult case. *At 5 a.m., the night watchman woke me up to say there was a man at the back gate who need help immediately. He was a Turk, the watchman said, but the Turks wouldn't take him in. I dressed quickly and sent the watchman to awaken Dr. Bellson. When I approached the man, he was holding his face in his hands. It had been partly torn off by a jackal, according to the watchman. With each hand, the man was holding a cheek in its rightful place. Blood was streaming down below his fingers. With everyone working together, we prepared him for the operation in less than ten minutes. The man is comfortable in bed now. His face is swathed in bandages with two catheters sticking up like tiny periscopes so he can breathe. Another tube goes down his throat for feeding. When I go to him and speak, he reaches out to take my hand.*

Winter 2014

Peter sleeps on and off. *Sirens and smoke at 2. Dreamed Stephen asked me to stand in for him in a play that featured an elaborate set with Middle Eastern pointed archways. He handed me a three-pointed sword and told me to joust. Some guy in a 1970s leisure suit demanded I atone for my sins. The sword flew out of my hands and entered my stomach. Luckily, I woke up. Took my temperature: 101. Stomach's a lot better. Stephen said he would have never felt the need to cheat, if I weren't so straight-laced and predictable. Wasn't so predictable when I shouted the word AIDS, after he told me I was boring in bed. He's right, though. Sex is no good, when all you can think about is disease, especially when it's not there. Slept another hour. Dreamed of fundamentalist Christians protesting at the funeral of an American soldier killed in action. These people really exist—those who blame gay men for the loss of soldiers' lives. Read about them in the paper. Fever up to 103. Joe and Fran here. Taking me to the hospital.*

Spring 1994

Peter graduates from college with a degree in professional writing and no debt, thanks to his grandmother's annuity, alongside his job selling vacuum cleaners. At his graduation party, his parents give him a framed picture of his grandmother at age 25. Sitting atop Chochuk, a horse she used to ride around the streets of Smyrna, the young nurse with close-cropped bangs looks down into the camera, her eyes wide, spine erect. *I wish I could have known her,* says Peter. She really loved you, says his mother. Peter claims no recollection of his grandmother. His mother shakes her head and says she wishes that love wasn't something that had to be recollected.

His father offers to take him on a pleasure trip to Europe, just the three of us, he says. Peter declines, says he wants to focus on finding a full-time job as a professional writer. His mother and father go on the trip without him. Peter gets a well-paying position writing operation manuals for vacuum cleaners and other appliances.

Spring 1919

Grace dances with Dr. Bellson. *It was a grand affair, and I loved every minute, especially when he lowered me into the most elegant dip. Helped him with a difficult case of appendicitis, and he took me for a walk to the top of Mount Pagus. From there we viewed the ruins of the Greek and Roman Theater and Polycarp's tomb. Dr. Bellson and I talked and talked. He loves eating strawberry ice cream, playing whist, and riding his motorcycle on Cape Cod. I called him Son of Alexander Graham, and he laughed. We both miss home.*

I felt a slight chill in the air, and the good doctor gave me his jacket. Then he told me to make sure to dress properly when I ride Chochuk. Said people might start calling me Lady Godiva if I didn't. I couldn't stop blushing. Not sure how I feel about the comment. If I were back home, I would have slapped his face. Here, where ladies do not need a chaperone to walk with a gentleman, I am not sure how to react.

There is a rumor going around about Dr. Bellson and me. After last night's shift, he told me about it. Said the others didn't understand our platonic friendship. I agreed. We both decided to spend less time together aside from work. Cried myself to sleep.

Winter 2014

Peter suffers a burst appendix. *Sepsis. IV drip, tons of medication. Nurses with needles won't leave me alone. Machine bleeps when my blood pressure gets low.*

A bit better. Mom brought the newspaper. Dad stayed home because he has bronchitis. Front-page picture of Stephen—mouth open, spittle on his lip. Definitely shouting. Love to know what he's saying. Article says protest got out of hand, people arrested.

Fall 1993

In order to fulfill requirements for his undergraduate writing major, Peter takes a journalism course, for which he must choose a local business, interview an employee, and write a feature article about the business. He chooses a housecleaning company, where he meets Stephen, who says, *Come shadow me for the afternoon.* When Stephen's vacuum cleaner breaks down, Peter fixes it by bending, twisting, and jiggling a set of poorly designed parts. *Not bad for a brainy college student,* says Stephen, who invites Peter to dinner. They agree to meet again, next time at a dance club. Peter receives an A on his assignment.

Winter 1920

Grace plans a trip to Proti to meet a ship full of refugees. *Heavy snow and blizzard. Admiral Bristol said he would send his yacht up the Bosporus for me. So, in the middle of the storm I started down the long hill to the quay. Couldn't make it. Came back and phoned headquarters and was told the ship could not make it either! Was told the car would come for me the following morning, but I would have to meet it at the bottom of the hill. Met the car but not without freezing my feet. Never have I felt so cold, not even at home in New Hampshire.*

Found out that the ship with refugees was still floundering on the Black Sea. We shoved off, and then a few yards from the quay, couldn't see more than a foot off the boat. Soon the captain didn't know where he was. *The trip should have taken an hour, but instead took six. We had to drop anchor quite a way offshore and had to ride in a rowboat to the dock in a furious storm. I fell in, and a sailor rescued me.*

Slept in our coats last night but still nearly froze. Refugees arrived. Then came a destroyer with beds and other supplies. Refugees in bad shape. Women sick with either pneumonia or typhus. We all helped with moving them off the ship, and I stood and dished up mugs of soup until my arm hurt senseless. Work is nonstop but so necessary. Got to bed at 12:30 and couldn't fall asleep thinking about those so unfortunate. My foot hurting something terrible. Thinking about the refugees, I found the pain superfluous. So many in such awful condition. Wounds alive with maggots, heads full of lice. Malnourished and mentally broken by unbelievable horrors.

Winter 2014

The doctor puts Peter on soft food. *Happiness short-lived. Diarrhea: just writing the word makes me never want to eat again. No one can come into my room without putting on gloves and a gown. Precaution so my infections don't spread. Feel like a leper. A young nurse named Brie was horrified when she had to take the bedpan. Who names their kid after cheese? Wonder what happened to the lady I used to be friends with at the historic house. Forgot her name.*

Last night Mom sat on the edge of the bed and told me about her mother working in a hospital in Turkey. At 25, my grandmother assisted an appendectomy in a city under siege. Whole building was shaking during the operation. Every movement she and the doctor made required intense concentration and precision. When Mom left, I turned out the light and imagined my grandmother holding ether over my mouth while a doctor dug out my burst appendix, bed jolting and bouncing as mortar shells shook the hospital walls.

Bad day. Potassium drip. Pain so sharp, bit through tongue. Couldn't help it. Nurse stopped drip. Arm and stomach a little better. Going over dance steps in head to get mind off pain and break up monotony.

Winter 1979

To break the monotony of being snowbound for a week, Peter's mother and father decide to clean the house. At 7, Peter is allowed to use the little vacuum cleaner, which has a wedge-shaped piece to clean corners. Peter turns the switch on and off twice without plugging in the vacuum. His father tells him the appliance will not work without electricity. Peter tells his father he knows all about electricity, that he turned the switch on and off on purpose to warn the little people that he was going to clean the floors. *Then they can get out of the way,* he says. His father asks who the little people are. Peter tells him, *They are invisible miniature humans, one assigned to every average-sized human to make sure the person lives a happy life.* His mother asks where he first heard about the little people, *a cartoon or a book?* Peter says he made them up on his own, after falling asleep on the living room carpet during the news. He dreamed the little people ended the Vietnam War by making normal and big-sized humans too happy to fight. *The little people jumped around and wiggled their hips so the big people couldn't help but laugh.* Peter's father assures his son that little people do not exist. Peter asks his mother to tell a story, the one about how she gave up her job to have a baby. *Come dance with me,* says Peter's mother. Peter's father puts disco music on the stereo, and mother and son make indentations in the carpet, as they skitter across the floor, jumping, laughing, and wiggling.

Winter 1920

A little after 2 a.m., Grace screams. *The girls got Dr. Bellson, and he said I had frozen my foot and had neglected it. He dressed it with icthyol ointment and then gave me a sedative. Assured me I would be fine. I wish he liked me as much as I like him.*

Winter 2014

A nurse and her assistant take out Peter's drains. *Eternity of pain—two tubes sliced through my guts. Nearly made the nurse deaf. Back on morphine. Mom came by with a book: Grandmother's diary. Too weak to read.*

Winter 1973

Grace has an argument with her daughter about dressing the baby to go outside. *His feet must be kept warm,* she says, *even if he's out for just a few minutes.* Susan lets out a hiss. *He's not trudging through a snowstorm on his way to help refugees,* she says. *We all know your story. You've told it a thousand times. Don't you think it's time to let it go? Not everyone who goes out on a winter day is going to get frostbite.* Grace gives the baby a kiss on the forehead and mutters something about his sensitive nature. She says nothing to her daughter as she leaves. This is the final interaction between mother and daughter, before mother dies.

Winter 2014

Still hooked to an IV, Peter starts his grandmother's diary, which begins with her boat trip to Turkey. He tries to imagine what it was like for a single woman to break conventions and travel so far, live such an exciting and dangerous life nearly a hundred years ago. He cries when he gets to the parts that deal with poverty and war.

Joe and Fran come for a visit. Instead of bringing flowers, they present Peter with a DVD of a folk-dance festival in Riga, Latvia. They watch Ukrainian men dressed in red boots and white shirts with colorful brocade drop to their knees and kick their legs with great speed and scissor-like precision. *My Ukrainian ancestors settled in Latvia after Ukraine was decimated by the Russians,* says Joe, who then tells Peter about *the Holodomor,* Joseph Stalin's starvation of nearly seven million Ukrainians in the early 1930s. Joe's face becomes red when he utters the name *Stalin.* Peter mentions the Armenian Genocide. Joe and Fran leave a few minutes later, and Peter reads the rest of his grandmother's diary.

When his mother visits, Peter thanks her for the diary. She says she's only read parts because the book brings up memories she doesn't want to deal with. *Like what?* asks Peter. His mother says that she and her brother had winter and summer sets of shoes when they were growing up. Two different sizes, the winter shoes big enough to house their feet, along with three pairs of heavy socks. The silver fillings in Peter's mother's teeth sparkle, as she utters the word *socks*. *I always resented my mother*, she says, *for forcing us to wear so many pairs of socks. I resented her as long as she lived.* Peter asks his mother if the resentment is gone. She says she's not sure, yet she feels guilty for her anger. Peter tells his mother that Stephen feels the same toward him for growing up privileged, for being so particular. Before his mother can respond, he asks if she wishes she had gone back to work after he was born. She says no.

He then asks if she knows what happened to Dr. Bellson. She tells him the doctor went to Marash with two thousand Turkish gold lire to help supply food to the nearly ten thousand Armenian refugees and orphans. *Makes me feel foolish for worrying about little things*, says Peter. *This was the last correspondence between Grace and Dr. Bellson*, says his mother. *Your grandmother remembered exactly what the good doctor told her about those times. Used to repeat it, when she was angry with Father. What did he say?* asks Peter. *Even if you didn't know where you were going, you could easily find your way between Islahiyé and Marash by following the line of skeletons along the path.* Peter calls Dr. Bellson a hero.

Peter's mother tells him that her brother has a theory that the doctor was gay. Peter asks her if she agrees, and she says it makes sense, but doesn't really know. *Your grandmother and I gradually grew apart. She stopped confiding in me. Once, not long after you were born, there was a TV news segment on homosexuality. My mother quickly turned it off.*

Peter's mother continues to talk, but he loses concentration. The painkillers have begun to wear off, and he doesn't want to think of his grandmother as a homophobe. His abdomen reacts with a sudden jolt, and Peter remembers a story from Grace's diary, about the man whose face had been ripped off by a jackal—the Turk who was turned away from the Turkish hospital. As Peter's mother continues to speak, he thinks of the day he asked Stephen, his only boyfriend, to move in with him.

It was right after Stephen had told him the story of two men picking him up at a bar and inviting him to their place. When Stephen got into their car, they told him they were straight. Then they beat him up. They might have killed Stephen, if he hadn't escaped—face, arms, and legs bleeding, clothes torn off. The police refused to take him seriously, not in his blue bikini underwear. They called him a prostitute, even though it wasn't true. Nobody's safe anywhere, mutters Peter. His mother asks what he said, and he says it's nothing. She follows up with a question about his plans for a future without Stephen. Peter says he has no plans, then pushes the button to call the nurse, who comes quickly and replenishes his painkillers. The nurse leaves, and Peter's mother tells him she has a better remedy for his pain. *What would that be?* asks Peter. The little people, she says. Peter laughs. As the medicine takes effect, he begins to feel sleepy. *Come to folk dancing,* he says, *when I'm better. Come dance with me.*

Origin

Introduction

Long before humankind arrived on Earth, there was Dance. A state of eloquence encased in a spark of spontaneity, Dance set the world in motion. When it was happy, Dance swayed with the birds to the tune of a breeze. When it was angry, Dance shook the Earth with thunder, temblors, and tornadoes. A partner to shearwaters skimming the foam, Dance moved with agility and grace, a prequel to a male ballet dancer performing a *pas de deux*—dominant yet deferent, honoring its partner over itself. Dance had a rhythm so synchronized, that the Earth *couldn't ask for anything more.*

Achievement

When Dance was not dancing, it served as a trainer and artistic director, teaching life-altering movements to all creatures, making sure that they evolved. On one hand, Dance enabled a lion to alight upon the back of a gazelle, and on another, it assisted a gazelle to sidestep the pursuit of a lion. In rehearsal, Dance explored its association with Earth and its inhabitants. Dance worked closely with Wind to water the world, with Fire to form islands. But Dance was far from perfect. In one instance, it enabled a herd of wooly mammoth to run faster by showing them a new way of curving their trunks. The tactic worked well, especially when it came to capturing prey. But Dance failed to consider the visual impairment resulting from such a move. The herd fell into a giant hot spring and scalded themselves to death. Despite such a setback, Dance worked hard to perfect its craft.

Creativity

When all was well and Dance had nothing to do, it separated into three parts—extensions, jumps, and turns—and danced with itself. When it got bored, it created dances with inanimate objects, a favorite involving dead leaves. With the help of the wind, Dance sent the leaves skyward in a leaping, swirling flourish. Then, as a gesture toward Gravity, it let the leaves drift down through the branches they once inhabited. When the game was over, Dance merged into one, allowing itself to pause long enough to pose questions about its purpose, about the lives of plants and living creatures, about the cycles of birth and death.

Despite the leaf game and others like it, Dance failed to find answers and eventually got tired—of the Earth, of its job, of itself. As a result, Dance began to neglect its work and spent most of its time separated in parts. Extensions wanted to extend, jumps to jump, and turns to turn, each in different directions. This was when The Great Choreographer, Dance's originator, stepped down from its dais. A form of energy encased in mystery, the Great Choreographer acted as a nerve, like a spark of electricity on the backbone of an inkling, to help Dance put itself back together. But Dance failed to perform as before. Its movements were no longer in harmony.

Failure
Dance stopped. Temperatures cooled. Dinosaurs died.

Birth
On a bleak and frigid day, in which the only movement Dance could muster was a shiver, it received a gift from The Great Choreographer. From high in the stratosphere came an aurora borealis of sparks—extending, jumping, and turning in the sky. The sparks landed on Dance, which grew heavy and round. An iridescent ameba, barely able to roll itself into the recesses of a cave, Dance went to sleep, along with the rest of the Earth and its inhabitants. The sleep lasted a year, during which the sparks developed. On the thirty-first day of the twelfth month, temperatures rose; snow and ice melted; and trees sprouted, bloomed, and bore fruit.

The next day Dance gave birth to the first people—identical triplets, full-grown and green as chameleons camouflaged on a moss-covered log. Their birth was the first dance performed by humans. Slow and tentative, the triplets extended their arms, felt the air, discovered one another. Mesmerized by the grandeur of touch and the freedom of movement, they tested every muscle and joint, bending and stretching, finding an embrace, reveling in stillness. Dance was ecstatic. Resuming its place in the world, Dance rejoiced with a breeze.

Development

Named by anthropologists as Flourish, Gesture, and Pose, the triplets possessed no sexual organs. Their well-developed calves and quads resembled present-day male *Homo sapiens*, while their protruding breasts and long necks appeared female. Although Pose favored extensions, Flourish turns, and Gesture jumps, each was able to perform the three categories of moves instinctively. Living in a tropical climate, the triplets needed no clothes. Although they sometimes had their differences— Pose savored moments of quiet, while Flourish preferred flamboyance, for example—the triplets got along well. They worked amicably to survive and enjoy life. Using stones, along with a series of grand movements, Flourish hunted animals. A talented communicator with a penchant for exploration, Gesture created a language of pantomime to convey its discoveries in the surrounding wilderness. A deep thinker with a natural ability to organize, Pose choreographed intricate schedules that balanced pleasure with work. Something—nobody knows what—about the triplets' movements kept them safe from predators.

Threat

After three years, the triplets had created a vast repertoire of dances—some to ward off wild animals, others to give thanks for an abundance of meat, and still others to express playfulness and camaraderie. During the fourth year, Pose assumed an extended series of poses, not unlike those one might eventually see in a musical choreographed by Bob Fosse. Flourish and Gesture reacted with a flurry of jumps and turns. Night fell, and the three were heady with laughter. Suddenly, the Earth shook. Pose ducked, barely escaping a falling tree. Gesture reached, as the land below gave way. And Flourish spiraled and flailed to the edge of a meadow. Horrified and surprised by the violent movement created by an unknown force, Dance searched for the cause of the earthquake.

Separation

A rift—ten feet wide and twenty feet deep—had separated the triplets. Pose ended up on one side, Flourish on the other, and Gesture at the bottom of the chasm. With the exception of a few bruises, each was all right. Performing a series of dance solos simultaneously, the triplets learned each other's general locations. They had developed a form of ESP enhanced by their dancing. Despite their inability to reunite during a lengthy period of aftershocks, the three had hope.

Discovery

At the end of a fortnight, heavy fog steamed up through the rift. Overcome with worry and fear, Pose sat silently at the edge of the chasm, trying to figure a way down to Gesture. Frustrated and angry, Pose performed an experimental dance not unlike what eventually would become the hokey pokey. In the midst of shaking all about, Pose learned to translate pantomime into sounds. Gesture heard and interpreted the sounds, which indicated that Gesture should search for a long vine to throw to Pose. Within an hour, the two were reunited at the top of the chasm.

For a week Pose and Gesture worked to match sounds with meaning, each calling out once an hour to determine the exact location of Flourish. In the midst of this experiment, the two had begun to create the world's first language—words borne out of necessity, of movement and passion, of an interpretation of Dance.

Strife

Meanwhile, Dance scoured the world in search of the cause of the temblor. In a clap of thunder, it found the answer: Dissonance, a natural byproduct of all movement. A lover of harmony, Dance refused to acknowledge Dissonance, which became ecstatic, for Dance's refusal served as proof positive that Dissonance was a part of Dance, as well as its progeny.

Dance and Dissonance argued. They disagreed about priorities, Dance promoting unity and simplicity, and Dissonance fostering diversity and complexity. Unlike verbal dialogue, the argument involved a series of movements, none of which could be considered graceful or sustained. Dance claimed that only with cooperation and a positive attitude could the triplets survive and succeed. Dissonance claimed that only with dissatisfaction and conflict could they develop and evolve. This argument serves as a model for interlocutions among a variety of political figures. Dissonance and Dance argued so long and hard that they caused another earthquake, this one closing the rift.

Reunion

When the Earth settled down, Flourish came home. The triplets were reunited. At first, Flourish failed to recognize Pose, whose skin had turned a pale, grasshopper green. A similar case occurred with Pose and Gesture, who feared that Flourish had been invaded and burnt, its muscles so developed and complexion so dark. This is the first known occurrence of racism. When the three embraced, Flourish felt Pose's bones protruding from its nearly translucent skin. Flourish's embrace was so forceful that Pose retracted in pain. Flourish didn't know how to react, so it changed the subject by dancing its adventures. It was proud to convey how it had tied a sharp rock to a stick to throw at prey, but Pose and Gesture had nearly forgotten the old language of pantomime.

Scholarship

For the next month, Pose and Gesture taught Flourish how to speak, and Flourish taught Gesture and Pose how to hunt with its new device. Their time for dancing diminished. Gesture and Pose grew further apart, each claiming authorship of the new language, while Flourish kept peace by praising its siblings. Oftentimes, Flourish added a variety of exaggerations and nuances to its speech, making Pose and Gesture laugh, but tensions between rivals continued to heighten. Not until Gesture fell down and lost its ability to gesticulate did the rift begin to heal. Pose became quite solicitous, feeding its sibling and creating a healing dance—movements of contraction and release that would eventually enter the choreography of modern dance matriarch Martha Graham. By the time Gesture was well, hard feelings had gone away. Gesture was grateful and grew closer to Pose, but Flourish felt left out and resented the reunion. Pose and Gesture agreed to make Flourish feel more included, but not until it was too late: Flourish had left.

Fruition

Miles away, Flourish became bored and depressed, losing its desire to kill animals for food. With the help of Dissonance, who entered Flourish's stomach, the triplet learned the difference between edible and poisonous plants in its new environment. Flourish amused itself by playing a game, in which it spat seeds into a small hole. When the seeds sprouted plants, and the plants bore fruit, the sibling's spirits began to lift. Flourish had become Earth's first farmer.

Lonely and sad, Pose and Gesture set out to find Flourish but separated and got lost, neither able to summon the energy to perform their ESP dance. Thanks to body memory, each retraced old movements and made it back to the cave, hoping the third sibling would return eventually.

Devotion

During the month they waited, Pose and Gesture developed the belief that movement and thought could affect the outcome of an event. This conviction reflects the world's first religion. Praying that their sibling would return soon, the two held each other's right hand while facing in opposite directions. Then they extended their free arms while rotating slowly, pivoting on the right foot. When they completed a circle, they paused, knees bent, faces lifting toward the sky. They held the pose long enough to utter Flourish's name. After the world's first liturgical dance came to a close, Pose and Gesture gained a greater appetite for meat, using Flourish's spears to hunt. Pose put out bait for hungry animals and hid in a nearby copse, while

Gesture speared them to death.

Forgiveness

A week's walk away, Flourish engaged in its own dance, as it placed seeds in holes it had dug with its toes. During its time in the wilderness, Flourish had planted a garden and a small orchard. Killing only the animals that bothered its plants, Flourish had lost its appetite for meat. A vegetarian, it had grown leaner. Spending most of its time gardening in the sun, Flourish developed an even deeper skin tone. At night, Flourish practiced Gesture and Pose's language until it fell asleep.

Flourish soon made its way back to the cave, and the triplets rejoiced with a variety of moves, sounds, and words. Then they moved to Flourish's farm and built a lean-to, big enough for three. They hunted, farmed, and danced, treating each other with dignity and respect.

Evolution

A year later, the triplets choreographed and performed a most unusual dance. Turning on their knees not unlike Chinese classical dancers thousands of years later, they headed to a nearby watering hole, slogging in mud, laughing as they danced. When they reached the edge of a pond, its face speckled with water lilies, its underbelly teeming with fish, they joined hands and dove. Rolling, tumbling, and sprinting beneath dry land, they shimmered with iridescence as they performed the world's first water ballet. Although the triplets eventually returned to the surface, they did not survive. Their sacrifice was necessary for the evolution of humankind.

The Great Choreographer sent down a series of sparks, which entered the corpses of Pose, Gesture, and Flourish, causing them to roll back beneath the pond's surface. Nine months later came the first men and women, borne out of these bodies, full grown and swimming. It is from this lineage that many of us come—great thinkers from Pose, great communicators from Gesture, great athletes from Flourish. Last, we have the great troublemakers, borne not of the triplets, but of the relationship between Dance and Dissonance, destined to create complexity in the lives of all who try to get along, all who dedicate themselves to an ideal, to a divine sense of movement that radiates when humans truly Dance.

Poisoning the Dick

You know they don't allow you to have shoes in mental hospitals. That's why they give you a stack of socks—industrial quality, turquoise for women, socks with little white rubber treads on the bottoms to keep you from falling in the halls when the meds take effect. Whenever I think of socks, I'm reminded of a 20-something patient named Giselle. Not long after we met in the halls of the hospital, Giselle told me that "you can really feel the metatarsal arches when practicing in socks." Feeling the metatarsals is a prerequisite for pointing the feet, according to Giselle, whose tight, fit body challenges anyone stupid enough to question her statement. When she engages her ankles to form two perfect points, her feet remind me of curved medieval sabers I saw at an art auction—a warning to get out of the way when she executes a move. Giselle is a professional ballerina: blood-red hair, green eyes, and the body of an action figure come to life. No nineteenth-century porcelain fragility in her bones. Muscle and speed, brains and wit: that's how I think of Giselle. How else could she have gotten away with poisoning her director and coming to an exclusive private mental hospital instead of going to jail or prison?

Our first meeting was rather tense. It was my second day as a patient, and I was just getting used to walking around in my turquoise socks. The shrink had told me to take note of the things that bother me, learn to pace myself in order to avoid another breakdown. For fear that I would be offended by everything anyone might say, that I could never live up to the doctor's standards, I had yet to speak to another patient. Making my way through the hallway, not bothering anyone, I found myself blocked by a pair of long, lithe legs.

"Keep walking like that, and you'll never get out of here." Those were the first words the bitchy ballerina spat in my face. Then she let out a cigarette-smoke sigh that activated my allergies. "It looks like you're doing the thorazine shuffle," she said. "You'll end up a zombie if you don't watch out."

I said nothing, not until I finished sneezing and blowing my nose. "You're not allowed to smoke in the building," I whispered, trying to take note of the relationship between my shaking body and the indignation I felt toward the stranger before me.

Not saying a word, Giselle tapped the back of her head with the tip of her toe. "I do what I want," she added. "Life's more fun that way."

I took a deep breath. "Then why not let others do what *they* want," I said, "like walking in peace?"

Giselle looked down at my legs and said my shuffling was hardly an expression of tranquility. "In fact," she noted, "that walk, if you performed it out on the street, is more likely to get you mugged or raped."

I took a step toward the woman. "Thorazine was replaced long ago at mental hospitals," I said, trying to regulate my breath. "If anyone has lost her mind, it's you, not me. Perhaps you damaged your brain the last time you kicked yourself in the head." Hunched and panting, I began to walk away, but I stopped when Giselle started laughing.

"You talk like a dancer," she said. "I'll bet I can teach you some ballet."

And so she did. The 5-foot-7-inch, 117-pound ballerina who nearly poisoned her director to death taught me a lot more than ballet during the six months I spent at the hospital. She not only helped me exercise but also took my mind off my husband and mother-in-law, the people who made me feel crazier than I actually was. She even taught me a bit of science—everything from the anatomy of a dancer's body to the physiology of caustic ingestion. But first came the basics of ballet. Instruction was intense, with two-hour classes, in which I bent, stretched, and twisted parts of my body I never knew existed. And by the time Giselle got through with me, I wished they didn't. With the dancer exhaling residual smoke in my face, I learned to *plié, tendu, rond de jambe,* and *fondu.*

Fondues and *rond de jambes* are especially significant for Giselle, for it was in the midst of performing these steps that she had gotten the idea to poison her director. I was finishing my first week of classes, when she revealed her passion for one particular poison.

128

"Very elegant and classical," she said, describing the pretty purple flowers produced by the bella donna plant. Then she went into detail about the importance of her choice: "Long ago, Italian women knew how to use the poison without hurting themselves. They squirted the juice of the bella donna berry in their eyes. Dilated pupils were most appealing to men."

The more the ballerina talked, the more comfortable I felt. Her voice was soothing yet ominous—something to listen to with full attention.

"Bella donna means 'beautiful woman,' " she said. "One way or another I was going to prove to my director that *I* am a beautiful dancer."

I asked Giselle how she knew so much about plants, and she told me her grandmother was an herbalist. Then she swatted my shoulder, insisting that I concentrate on my *fondues*. A *fondu* is a move that's supposed to simulate the act of melting. Bend both knees, allowing one foot to come to rest in a pointed position at the ankle—sounds easy, but you try doing it fifty times, just to hear the belligerent ballerina tell you that you did it wrong and had to "do it again." But, as Giselle insisted, dancers must have discipline in order to succeed—discipline and a lot of patience.

During my second week of classes, I got the rest of the story. Giselle was rehearsing a solo, when director Dyklan Voss—think Dylan with a *k*—first whispered in her ear.

Synchronize was the word he used. "Not a bad correction for a principal dancer learning the role of Princess Aurora," said Giselle. "Quite apropos." It's the man's tongue in her ear in the midst of the whisper she failed to appreciate. "But I knew if I said something, The Dick might give Aurora to Betsy Beacon. I'd have rather gotten raped."

Giselle said she has dreamed of becoming Aurora, known to the non-ballet world as the Sleeping Beauty, since she was 5. Then she explained that directors use their knowledge of dancers' hopes and dreams to play mind games. For example, cast lists can change in a moment, which means an understudy like Betsy could end up with the role of Aurora, if Giselle were to say or do something displeasing to her director.

According to Giselle, Dyklan Voss never got the chance to

rape her.

"How did you avoid it?" I asked, having seen the director on TV several years back.

With biceps like eggplants and calves that reminded me of bear cubs clinging to the trunks of trees, I couldn't imagine anything but consent or rape.

"I let him come close," Giselle whispered so softly I got goose bumps. Then she went into detail about how she lured the director into her trap. First she purchased an exclusive cube of Belgian dark chocolate, which she melted in a double boiler over a low flame, before dabbing it with a sterilized sable paintbrush just inside her right ear. A connoisseur of cacao, Voss grew even fonder of licking the ballerina's aural cavity. But as time went on, whispered corrections were replaced by snide remarks about Giselle's dancing. Yet the more the director criticized, the more the dancer indulged in decorating her ear with layers of Becolade, imported from Brussels.

"My original intention was to get him hooked and then mix the chocolate with a tiny bit of poison, only enough to get him to hallucinate and stumble around," said Giselle. "Then I could play nursemaid and end up dancing Aurora."

But when Dyklan told her she looked as if she were scratching her asshole with her big toe, as she performed Aurora's *rond de jambe* in *plié en pointe*, the ballerina went berserk.

"I made a mini-truffle the size of a pearl and filled it with poison," she said. "All it took was a dab of spirit gum to stick the candy in my ear." Giselle nodded. "By the time he finished licking, The Dick landed flat on his ass."

When Giselle finished telling the story of poisoning The Dick—the director had a seizure and had to be rushed to the hospital—I laughed so hard I lost my voice. Not until I got a month into my lessons with the ballerina did I begin to understand the social dynamics of ballet—how world-class professional dancers and directors interact: one minute so elegant and polished, and the next writhing on the floor, foaming at the mouth, shouting obscenities, both dancer and director, in some cases. Of course I didn't help things, not when I took the role of ballerina, and Giselle the director. How I didn't see what was coming, I don't know. Yes, I do. I was blinded by movement searing through my bones, dripping with adrenaline as I learned what it feels like to *sauté, changement, emboîté*—flying through the air, reaching for perfection. Ballet: dance at its purest, the most refined form of movement a human will ever perform. At least now I know why people put their bodies through hell to train day and night for a low-paying job that lasts not much longer than a decade and ends in serious injury or insanity for some. Ballet: poorly funded and ignored by mainstream society, laughed at among the youth who'd rather play sports, take drugs, and fuck. But if becoming a professional dancer is half as thrilling as what I experienced when studying with Giselle, I'd go back in time thirty years, move to Communist Russia, and dedicate my life to becoming a ballerina, even if all I ever achieved was a space in the back corner of the *corps de ballet*.

When I took the role of Giselle's pupil-protégé, the two of us bonded. We entered a space in which the physical, mental, and spiritual somehow merged in the midst of movement, divine intervention: Deus ex Machina dropping down to straighten my leg in an *assemblé*, guide my arms in a *port de bras*. Sure, Giselle had her hands all over me—squeeze this, tighten that—but all was in the name of ballet. Nothing was out of place. And although I'll never even be good enough to call myself an average student of this sacred art form, I know in my 35-year-old bones that ballet has made me into something that exceeds normal human existence. Unfortunately, that something comes with a price. And in my sixth month of lessons, when I finally snapped, I wasn't so graceful as the ballerina with the bella donna.

The eight weeks leading up to my most notable interaction with Giselle were as manic as the holiday season during which they fell. No time to notice the student-teacher relationship fraying at the edges, like the faded chiffon ballet skirt I was allowed to wear during practice. The hospital had joined the Christmas rush: new patients, less time with the shrink, and overworked orderlies, whose personalities, at times, resembled those of the people they were supposed to comfort. After a flurry of complaints of something burning, Giselle was caught smoking in the broom closet. But of course she managed to strike a deal with the head nurse to make up for her indiscretion by putting on a show. Without asking, she volunteered yours truly to serve as her dance partner in the Arabian Coffee *pas de deux* from Act II of *The Nutcracker*. By then, five months into my training, I was addicted enough to ballet to accept a man's role, in which I had to heft around a banshee who screamed every other second when I didn't put my hands in the right place, when I failed to straighten my arms on the count of six, or when I wobbled while supporting her hips during a series of pirouettes.

Partnering, which I didn't begin to learn until after the deal was made, is hard enough for a man, but for me, it was impossible. Even when I took notes about what to do, when to do it, and, most importantly, how not to get upset, I failed.

"I watered down the choreography, so even an idiot beginner could do it," snapped Giselle, after a two-hour rehearsal, in which I learned how to wrap my right arm around the ballerina's abdomen and my left over her leg in arabesque, all while carrying a heavier-than-expected body across the room. "I'm supposed to be flying over your head in a press lift," said Giselle, as I stood panting, my sweat forming a mosaic of droplets on the hardwood floor of the hospital gym. "What I've asked you to do is nothing."

When I caught my breath, I suggested we get a patient named Terry, restricted to a wheelchair, to take my place, if the choreography was easy enough to be called nothing. This was the first time I challenged Giselle since she had given me the part. Her reaction was quick: she whipped around and told me to go steal a cleaver from food services, so she could amputate my legs.

"You don't deserve to walk," she screamed.

Later that day, the ballerina made a trip to the kitchen, where she convinced the chef to make me a baked Alaska, my favorite dessert. I got through about two bites before Giselle sauntered into the dining hall, gave me a hug, and then snatched away the dessert.

"Need to make sure you fit your costume," she said. That night, before bed, she demanded that I perform a hundred crunches in order to ensure my stomach didn't stick out.

My debut as a dancer never happened. During the time patients are allowed to make outside calls on a landline, Giselle got a hold of one of her dance partners. He showed up with a couple of costumes, and the two performed Arabian Coffee, Giselle wearing a pair of pointe shoes strictly against hospital rules. Nurses, patients, doctors, and kitchen staff alike were so enamored that nobody said a word, including me. When the two performed the *pas de deux,* I felt ashamed, as if I had tread clumsily upon hallowed ground with my amateur attempts. Who was I to think I could lift another human, make her look as sacred as a saint? Another part of me was ecstatic to celebrate the achievement of two superhuman creatures performing acts of beauty that only the catatonic could fail to appreciate. Giselle came up afterward and introduced me to her partner Steve, told him I was responsible for helping her stay in shape.

I ended up making so many notes about my conflicting feelings that I didn't know what to think. In one version, I was a prop—existing solely to serve the dancer, to keep her motivated and busy, to remind her that I was not like her, that I represented the body and life of a mere human, someone to use, someone to fortify her ego with my mediocre sweat. What made me slightly more worthy than the average idiot was my interest in ballet, my willingness to fill a seat in the audience, my ability to recognize the greatness of a higher class of human. The shrink was no help, telling me to keep feeling, keep writing, keep taking my medication. All he did was call my husband and tell him to come visit. On Christmas Eve, my husband showed up—his first visit since I had entered the hospital in July. When he hugged me, I felt cold. Neither of us said very much. When he left after a half hour, I was relieved.

By the new year, Giselle had worked her magic to break as many rules as she pleased. In addition to smoking, she switched around sleeping arrangements, so that I was her latest roommate. Sleeping so close to the ballerina more than challenged the parameters of my limited and mundane experience. On a regular basis, I was granted the privilege of watching Giselle let Steve into our room late at night for fifteen minutes of sex. The monitors turned a blind eye, once Giselle had started teaching them exercises to lose weight. Of course I was too shocked at the sight of Giselle and Steve to move a muscle—watching two model specimens acting in unison, as if they were on stage, performing before an audience of salivating voyeurs. But despite their synchronistic cavorting, satisfaction was independent, as if each had retired into his or her own world, fulfilled not by one body giving another pleasure, but by the exhibition of executing lurid yet graceful moves that only dancers could perform during copulation. Who else but a male *danseur* would arch his back and look over his shoulder to see his bulbous buttocks in action, as he pressed his penis into his partner? Who else but a prima ballerina would wrap her legs around the body pulsating atop her own, just to watch her feet point? Not until I saw Giselle and Steve in action did I begin to understand the true meaning of narcissism.

A part of me wanted to be one of them—to feel what it's like to live in sleekness, the slippery ability to arouse anyone who walks by, to assume a sense of supremacy, to assign underlings to do my bidding. Giselle was Aurora, Arabian Coffee, and every other role she set her mind to perform. After I watched Giselle dance, Giselle have sex, Giselle tell people what to do, I felt as if I could go back to my boring, out-of-shape husband, get him in bed, and keep him going until he fell dead from a heart attack. Unfortunately, that's not what happened. Instead, I chose to keep dancing, studying with Giselle. But things were not the same, not since the ballerina put on a costume and danced before an audience at a private mental hospital. She no longer watched attentively when teaching me how to land softly from a jump, how to execute moves that required more strength and flexibility than a professional athlete could ever dream of achieving, never mind an administrative assistant at a no-name university. She was just like my boss and my husband—interested in me only to the extent that I filled my role. Prepare documents, cook dinner, perform *pliés*: it was all the same. Or was it?

Despite Giselle's lack of enthusiasm for my progression as a dance student, I became conscious that ballet was my medicine, the miracle drug that would enable me to be myself. When I delved into a *grand plié*, I was no longer performing a deep knee bend with my feet turned out; I had taken physical steps to examine my insides—what I was made of, why I had had a nervous breakdown after my chicken curry stir-fry splattered and stained my newly painted kitchen wall. I had begun to see myself from a distance: how I had spent my life doing what was expected of me. The lyrical, energetic, and complicated movements that ballet dancers perform every day to warm up enabled me to question everything from my marriage to my home. When I did a tendu combination, attempting mathematical precision to the front, side, and back with one leg and then the other, I saw my husband leaving his dishes on the table, day after day, as he went to watch the same TV shows from the same worn-out chair. When I performed *rond de jambes,* I saw the suburban tract house he picked out five years ago when we were first married, renovations planned and paid for by his generous mother.

"You better get rid of that curry stain before she comes over," my husband had said—the last thing he had said—before I purchased a can of glossy chocolate brown and redid the room.

I painted the curry stain, the refrigerator, the window glass. And then I painted myself.

Not until I had studied with Giselle for nearly six months did I realize that during my episode with the paint, I had started moving—not as precisely or beautifully as a dancer, but in a different direction, moving away from what felt comfortable, what failed to work. When my mother-in-law rang the bell, I moved in agony, as the dried latex pulled and cracked my skin. On my way to the ER, I moved away from the periphery, as the paint delved beneath my epidermis. As a mental hospital inmate and student of ballet, I moved into darkness.

It was the last week of January, while performing a *grand plié* in fourth—the most uncomfortable, twisted position out of five—when I started muttering about the events leading up to my hospital stay. Giselle was performing her own *grand plié,* humming Tchaikovsky's music for Arabian Coffee.

"Don't talk when you dance," she said, not even bothering to look up at me.

A second later, I had my first out-of-body experience. While squeezing my calloused fingers around the long, swan-like neck of the ballerina, I saw myself from a distance. It was as if I had split in two. One part of me was lying on my bed, passive and calm, as I gazed at the other part, strangling my struggling victim. Although the feeling in my hands was quite strong and pleasurable as I squeezed harder and harder, for a moment, I thought I was watching TV. I even contemplated changing the channel, not interested in seeing a somewhat out-of-shape brunette with split ends and paint-damaged skin using her body to destroy someone else's. Instead of feeling anger or sympathy, I took note of the crude and bombastic movements performed by both of us: my body hunched and pulsating, Giselle's twisted and flailing. No longer was the ballerina's body a work of art surpassing the limits of human capability—Terpsichore inspiring Euripides with angelic precision to the tune of Apollo's lyre. Suddenly, the woman was ordinary, performing a scene so many have seen too many times. As I watched my victim begin to lose her ability to struggle, I found myself wondering why humans love violence, when such actions depict the ultimate in ugliness. Having ingested my share of sadistic movies and shows, I had never experienced such disgust as I did when squeezing Giselle's neck. Never until these moments had I performed any greater violence than swatting flies. Not until I felt the heavy resistance of three orderlies grabbing my waist and arms did I return to my own body.

Giselle lived. When Dyklan Voss found out what happened, he rushed to the hospital. When the dancer's release papers were signed, the director carried her down the stairs and out the door. Giselle failed to press charges against me. Too busy rehearsing her role as Aurora for the company's upcoming performances of *Sleeping Beauty*. Steve would be her partner. After a month of close observation, I got a break from wearing my turquoise socks. Granted an evening's reprieve, I felt like Cinderella when I slipped into Giselle's left-behind purple stilettos and stepped into a cab. The ballerina had reserved a seat—front row center—for me to watch her get poisoned by the prick of a needle and saved by the kiss of a prince. Giselle and Steve received a five-minute standing ovation. After the performance, an usher escorted me to the ballerina's dressing room.

The Disco Heel

Studio 54

This is not the place for the bridge-and-tunnel crowd, suburbanites addicted to One a Day Vitamins, squares—people with no idea how to live. Even if they get past the velvet rope, they'll go bug-eyed on the banana leaf carpet, have a conniption fit when they confront their fatuous reflections in the mirrored burgundy walls. The flickering chase poles alone could put a Connecticut insurance salesman in cardiac arrest. And if a phony ever makes it as far as the dance floor, the poor square will freeze up the moment the crowd starts feelin' *the city breakin' and everybody shakin.'*

Getting in

To say that only the coolest cats get into Studio 54 is a lie. Even if you're the geekiest of nerds, all you have to do is freak out because *Le Freak c'est chic.* Take it from one Studio 54 aficionado who came up with a set of rules of entry. You can't get any geekier than he. Raised on stuffed cabbage in South Pittsburgh, Andrew Warhola spent his boyhood as a bedridden bag of nerves—a pale waif suffering from chorea, a twitchy nervous disorder that some call St. Vitus Dance. All the kid could do was twitch and draw pictures. But decades later here in New York, with his own art movement and a new name, Andy Warhol offers the following advice if you ever want to enter the glorious gates of Studio 54:

1. Show up either *with* or *in* Halston.
2. Arrive extremely early or extremely late.
3. Disembark from a mode of transportation—limousine, helicopter, or ambulance—that makes a statement.
4. Never wear polyester, especially when it comes to underwear.
5. Do not, for any reason, mention the name Andy Warhol.

A Big Fluke

Under no logical circumstances should Nina Macaluso and Matteo Grippi be allowed to enter Studio 54. The term geek is cool compared to these 18-year old natives of Pocono Pinnacle, Pennsylvania, on their first trip to the Big Apple. Not only are they wearing polyester—a pastel paisley dress for Nina and a robin's egg blue suit for Matteo—but they barely make it to the city in Matteo's rusty-green International Scout, whose defective exhaust powders their skin, clothes, and lungs with a gray layer of grit. Thanks to a lack of money, alongside Nina's idea to park for free in the middle of Manhattan on a Saturday night, they find a space an hour later on a dark street in Alphabet City.

Both are intoxicated on exhaust fumes—so much so that they fail to notice how dirty they look. Wait up, says Nina. I can't walk that fast in these damned shoes. Six-foot-two with the body of a college wrestler, Matteo says he's sorry, but fails to slow down. My legs aren't as long as yours, says Nina. We're halfway there, says Matteo, his hands clamped over his ears, as the subway rumbles from below. With dark brown, wavy hair not unlike that of the Marlboro Man, Matteo could pass for potentially cool, if it weren't for his hyperacusis, a disorder characterized by extreme sound sensitivity and intolerance. No, Matteo would not make it into the in-crowd, skirting the streets of New York like Quasimodo on steroids. With her petite frame and ample breasts, Nina might pass for hip, that is, if she knew how to walk properly in a pair of pumps. Every few steps, when an ankle starts to give way on a crack or bump, she stops. Yet both teens have potential, for they can perform all the latest disco moves, which they worked on for weeks, as they planned their escape to Studio 54.

Matteo finally manages to slow down, but not until it's too late, not until Nina catches her heel in a subway grate. Stop! she shouts, and Matteo comes to a halt. Mother of God, he says, rushing to her side. As he pulls on Nina's leg, a puff of warm air flows through the grate. Hurry up, says Nina. I think the subway's coming. Matteo pulls harder, and the rest of the shoe breaks free from the heel, still stuck in the grate. Matteo trips over Nina, causing her to fall sideways and scrape her knee. Shit, she says. Now I'm bleeding. Matteo apologizes, and asks Nina if she wants to turn around and go home. Not on your life, she screams. And I'm not leaving this spot without my heel. These shoes cost good money. With an Army knife, Matteo pries the heel loose and hands it to Nina. What am I supposed to do with that? she says. Is your ankle all right? asks Matteo, putting the heel in his jacket pocket. Yeah, says Nina. No thanks to you. Matteo grips Nina's hand as she bounces up and down, navigating the street with only one high heel.

After a few steps, she stops. This'll never work, she says. By the time we get there I'll have such blisters I won't be able to walk, never mind dance. Matteo suggests she take off both shoes, but Nina claims she might get a disease from walking shoeless on such dirty streets. I can carry you, says Matteo. No, says Nina, and they keep walking. When they turn the corner, Matteo spots a Pioneer Supermarket cart filled with plastic bags, smelly blankets, and pieces of cardboard. No way, says Nina. That dirty thing belongs to a bum, and I don't even want to go near it. I'll throw up. Matteo ignores her and tips over the cart, spilling out some of its contents. You want to get to Studio 54 or not? he says. Nina climbs in.

Making a Statement

Nina and Matteo and the grocery cart turn at a clip onto West 54th. Still half a block away from the club, they enter a space jammed with people waiting to get in. Matteo shouts, and a path appears. A woman dressed in a black-sequined jumpsuit, quite ensconced with the application of peach lip gloss, steps into the open space, and Matteo swerves to keep from hitting her. A homeless man, who has been chasing after the cart for the last eight blocks, also swerves, except when he makes the turn, he douses the woman with a long string of drool. The woman screams, and a man dressed in a white John Travolta suit laughs. A subway rumbles from below, causing Matteo to cup his hands over his ears and push the cart with his stomach.

Such is the visual statement Nina and Matteo make, when they arrive at Studio 54. While the homeless man runs away with his grocery cart, the two geeky teens from Pocono Pinnacle, Pennsylvania, are admitted to the club without delay.

The Initial Setup

Odd circumstances sometimes lead up to even odder outcomes. Take the following scenario, back in Pocono Pinnacle, a month before Nina and Matteo set foot in Studio 54.

Nina and her best friend Kristin go all the way to Scranton to get pastel paisley dresses for the high school dance. When they get back, they choose disco suits from a catalog for Kristin's boyfriend Matteo and Nina's boyfriend Joe—note who's dating whom. Kristin says, the expense will be more than worth it for the most exciting event in the history of this one-horse town. Not counting the polka nights at the Polish American Club, jokes Matteo. Half their senior class prefer rock to disco, so the friends prepare for a small turnout. Nina says she doesn't care, and the others agree. Even if it's just us, says Matteo, we're going to dance so long and hard, we'll shake the shuttle cars down in Benson's mine.

Nineteen of their classmates arrive for the dance—Kristin counts them. About ten minutes after the music begins, the power goes out. A loud car revs its motor outside the gym. It's the Deadheads, says Nina. When the lights come on, the dance resumes. Moments later Kristin smells a combination of pot and rubber and begins to sneeze. Matteo spots smoke coming from an overturned wastebasket. Donna Summer is singing *Spring Affair* when the alarm goes off. Members of the Pocono Pinnacle Volunteer Fire Department put out the fire, which produces a great deal of smoke and burns a stack of gym mats. This is the one and only time Kristin dances disco in public. *Mary Jane* started the fire, jokes one of the Deadheads the following week. When no one comes forward to admit to the arson, the principal cancels the senior prom. After parents protest, the principal resigns, but not until well into the summer. Nineteen Seventy-

Eight is the only year in the history of the high school that the senior prom is canceled.

When the four friends find out the news, Matteo calls a meeting—Joe can't make it—on the smokers' patio at school. Why don't we all drive to New York and go to Studio 54? he says. That's a great idea, says Nina, but Kristin shakes her head. I'd love to, she says, but my parents would never give me the money. Putting his hands on Kristin's waist, Matteo says, I'd be happy to pay. Kristin says no a second time, and Matteo leaves for his part-time job as a janitor at the Arthur Murray Dance studio. Nina says, Come on. There's nothing to worry about, and Kristin tells Nina to drop the subject. Nina says, It won't be the same without you. In the evening, Kristin receives a call from Matteo, who assures her he won't even try to kiss her, if she doesn't want him to. Just as long as we go to New York, he says. Nina's mother is even willing to vouch for you for the weekend. Kristin says no, and the two get into an argument. I'm not going to New York, says Kristin. Why? asks Matteo.

As one might guess, the conversation deteriorates from this point on. Kristin fails to give a reason, and Matteo keeps prodding. Maybe we shouldn't see each other anymore, if you can't respect my wishes, says Kristin. Maybe we shouldn't see each other any more, if you can't trust me, says Matteo. When both agree to break off the relationship, they hang up.

Getting Good

Anybody who knows anything about dance—from disco to ballet—will tell you that a successful dancer must have the right body, extraordinary talent, tremendous discipline, and a relentless desire to move with grace. Out of the three—Kristin, Matteo, and Nina—Matteo comes the closest to fulfilling these basic requirements. Long before he even heard of disco, Matteo was dancing—in the fields of his father's farm, in the woods behind the barn, anywhere he could. When he started his job as a janitor, he picked up steps while sweeping the floors, no instruction offered. Once he decided to exchange wages for lessons, he excelled. Second in line is Nina, who studied ballet for three years, has a fantastic memory for movement, and possesses enough talent to look good if she tries. However, she fails to understand the meaning of discipline and is more interested in having fun than working hard. Last of the bunch is Kristin, who has a great body, adequate sense of discipline, and decent memory, but limited talent. In other words, Nina can dance circles, squares, and parallelograms around Kristin, and Matteo knows it.

The Final Setup

The week after Studio 54 is suggested as an alternative prom site, Joe dumps Nina for a cheerleader who can't dance, and the trip gets canceled. The night they were supposed to go, Kristin stays over at Nina's, where the two drink wine, dance around the cellar, and imagine the trip that no one took. When Kristin cuts herself on the corkscrew, Nina says, Let's make a blood pact to stay friends for life, no matter how many boys or men come along and ruin things. Kristin says, Okay, but there's something I have to tell you. Even though I never want to see Matteo again, I trust him because he's a true a gentleman. What do you mean? asks Nina. Kristin lets out a sigh. It's okay here at home, but combine New York with Studio 54, and I might go all the way—no contraception, no thought about the future. Nina tells Kristin she's the most levelheaded person she's ever met. Matteo's probably not the guy for you, she says. Kristin asks Nina if *she's* interested in Matteo, and Nina says, No, he's not my type. Kind of strange, if you ask me.

The following day, when Matteo offers to drive Nina to Studio 54 for a Saturday night of feverish dancing, she no longer considers him all that strange. Why not? says Nina, as long as you know upfront, we're not dating, and I don't want to fool around. We'll come straight home from the club, Matteo promises. Only a night of dancing.

Also at Matteo's request, Nina and he practice disco after hours at the Arthur Murray Dance Studio every night for two weeks in preparation for their adventure to New York. We're still not dating, says Nina. I'm just doing this to go to Studio 54. I know, says Matteo. That's obvious. Kristin's still my best friend, says Nina. I know that, too, says Matteo. By the end of the two weeks, Nina is more excited about the trip than Matteo, who says he wants to get back with Kristin. She won't talk to me at school or take my calls, says Matteo. Give her time, says Nina.

The First Dance between New Friends

Kristin and Nina first become friends in second grade during a game of hopscotch. When Kristin gets a turn, she ends up putting two feet on square 3, and the other girls laugh at her, all except Nina. When Kristin runs away crying, Nina quits playing and comforts Kristin. You got to know which foot to put on which squares, says Nina. I don't think I can do it, says Kristin. I can teach you, says Nina. It's kind of like dancing. When Nina teaches Kristin how to play hopscotch, and Kristin wins three games in a row, the two girls agree to be best friends for life.

Inside Studio 54

A man dressed in pink artificial leopard-skin pants steps in front of Nina and Matteo, as they enter the lobby. Without uttering a word, the man sinks his fingers into Matteo's hair. Scrumptious, he says, as Matteo grabs the man's shoulder and pushes him away. Letting out a laugh, the man turns around and compliments Nina on her scraped knee. That's the most funkadelic sight I've seen all night. Grabbing onto Nina's shoulders and leading her farther into the room, Matteo turns her to face one of the towering mirrors. *Look* at us, he says. We got to get cleaned up. Nina examines her dress and lets out a gasp. What the hell happened? This'll never wash out. A tall redheaded woman wearing lime green thong underwear saunters by, and Nina grabs Matteo's belt loop. What do you have on underneath that suit? she asks. Black-and-white polka dot BVDs, says Matteo. Well, if that sissy boy can wear pink leopard pants, she says, you can get away with black-and-white polka dot BVDs. The two step aside and strip, Matteo into his piebald undies, and Nina into her noir Versace lace bra and panties, a birthday gift from her cousin in Italy. I can't believe we're doing this, says Matteo. Neither can I, says Nina.

Dancing at the Disco

The moment Nina and Matteo enter the dance floor, Studio 54 rushes into their blood. Chase poles blinking blue, green, and red lights lead their way, as the partners hustle through a throng of sweating bodies gyrating to a beat that simultaneously strokes and pummels the eardrums. Van McCoy sings, *do it,* and they do: step to the back, step to the front, rolling grapevine, Travolta. When the song is over, the couple settle by a circular metal sculpture of a sun, its eyes rolling with jeweled flashes. Neither speaks. His hands by his sides, Matteo holds his back straight. Despite the sound of people laughing and shouting to the music, his disorder has disappeared.

Barry Gibb starts to sing: *Oh, girl I've known you very well/ I've seen you growing every day/ I've never really looked before/ But now you take my breath away.* Matteo takes Nina's hand and plunges her into a dip. Arms interlock, feet pivot, and the two *make it shine.* As Matteo guides Nina into a half-turn rotation, he mouths, *oh, what a woman.*

Sex

His jacket draped over her shoulders on the walk back to the International Scout, Matteo carries Nina. When a subway rumbles from below, he fails to flinch, as he cradles his dance partner through the streets. You're cured, says Nina, thanks to Studio 54. Maybe, says Matteo. But if I'm cured, it's because of you.

When the vehicle fails to start, Matteo folds down the seat and spreads out a sleeping bag. The two begin to kiss. Suddenly, Matteo pulls himself away and tells Nina to sit tight while he finds an all-night drugstore. She says, I'll be waiting. When Matteo returns with a package of condoms, it's nearly twilight. In the middle of sex, Nina squeals, and Matteo jumps up and hits his head on the roof. Don't do that! he shouts. I can't *stand* that sound.

Nina and Matteo speak very little on the way back to Pocono Pinnacle. What we did was not supposed to happen, says Matteo, as they drive across the Delaware River. I know, says Nina, and it will never happen again. Both agree to keep the incident—the trip to New York, Studio 54, and, most importantly, the sex—a secret from Kristin. It would only hurt her, says Nina. You're right, says Matteo.

Dancing in the Snow

Three years before Kristin starts dating Matteo, the principal dismisses school two hours early because of an approaching blizzard. Five minutes into his drive home, Matteo recognizes Kristin's red Thunderbird fishtailing left and right, dancing all over the road as she attempts to descend a steep, curvy hill. When her car pirouettes into a ditch, Matteo stops his vehicle and approaches. The two are not friends, each having hung out with a different crowd. I can do it myself, says Kristin, using the brakes and gas pedal in an attempt to rock the car out of the ditch. You're going to flood the engine and burn up the tires, says Matteo. Good, says Kristin. I'd rather do that and stay stuck than be told what to do by a boy who's friends with a cheater. Before Matteo can respond, Kristin rolls up her window, shifts into reverse, and shoves the car onto the road.

The storm intensifies. As Kristin creeps along, Matteo follows at a distance, heavy snow blowing in circular torrents. She reaches the bottom of the steep road she lives on, before her car gets consumed by a snow bank. Matteo drives up slowly. Want a ride? he asks. Kristin rolls her eyes, before abandoning her car and getting into his vehicle. As the two head up the road, Kristin learns that Matteo is no longer friends with the boy who used to copy from her English tests. One thing worse than a cheater is someone who holds a grudge, says Matteo. Do that, and life turns black. Kristin looks at the way Matteo's mouth moves when he speaks. She imagines tracing her finger along his curly right sideburn and down to his lips. Matteo parks at the bottom of Kristin's driveway. Snow gathers on the windshield in clumps, as Matteo tells Kristin about his Uncle Gug, a farmer during the day and miner by night. For some reason, no one in the family talks to him, says Matteo. Kristin asks what he did wrong, and Matteo says he doesn't know. Maybe nothing.

The Dinner Date

A year before Matteo gets the idea to ask his friends to Studio 54, Kristin goes on her first date with him. He chooses a sit-down Italian restaurant forty miles away in Scranton. I've only eaten American food, says Kristin, so you should do the ordering. Playing with the collar of his button-down shirt, Matteo suggests pasta and sauce. You must have had pasta and sauce, he says, his hands flying up in the air and landing on the table with a thud. Kristin shakes her head. Where've you been? says Matteo. They serve spaghetti and meatballs—oh so grody—once a week in the school cafeteria. Kristin tells Matteo that she always brings a peanut butter and jelly sandwich for lunch. They order mostaccioli and marinara.

When the meal comes, Matteo crosses himself and says a prayer too softly for Kristin to hear. Brushing her shoulder with his muscular arm, he reaches for the jar of Parmesan cheese, which he then sprinkles over Kristin's plate of pasta in a flurry of shakes. You don't like this, and I'll take you straight home without kissing you, says Matteo. That's how sure I am you'll love authentic Italian cuisine. Kristin smiles and looks away. The two spend most of the meal discussing their interests. Matteo says he would love to visit New York, dance at a disco. Kristin says the city scares her, but she'd still like to come along, go to a Broadway show. Not until the waitress takes away the plates does Kristin tell Matteo she has just eaten the best meal she's ever tasted. Matteo invites her home for dinner. If you like *this* food, my mother's cooking will make you think you died and went to heaven. When it comes time to kiss Kristin, Matteo gets nervous and backs away. It's OK, says Kristin. I'll only bite if you want me to.

Nina's Influence

Nina, whose grandparents emigrated from Sicily, says the best way to get on the good side of an Italian family is to ask for seconds at dinner. Then they'll begin to warm up. Just make sure not to tell them you're Protestant. Kristin says she will neither overeat nor lie. Nina reminds Kristin of how *she* had lied by making up a false last name when introducing Nina to her parents. What's the problem? Nina shouts, connecting her fingertips to perform a series of shakes. Can't you pronounce Macaluso? Kristin reminds Nina that her parents don't like Italians. I was just trying to protect you, she says. And what do you think I'm trying to do? says Nina.

Meeting the Parents

At Matteo's parents' dinner table, Kristin says she belongs to the township's only Baptist church. Matteo's mother smiles and says, That's a very active congregation. Also smiling, his father asks Kristin if she has met any nice Baptist boys from her family's church. Kristin says, no, and I don't plan to. When Matteo and Kristin go outside, Matteo's mother and father start yelling at each other in Italian.

The Reconciliation

Two weeks after Nina and Matteo's excursion to Studio 54, Nina goes to Italy to visit relatives, and Kristin gets a job at a store two blocks away from the Arthur Murray Dance Studio. Matteo sees Kristin on the street, the two have dinner at the Italian restaurant in Scranton, and guess what? They get back together.

The Marriage

Having been promoted from unpaid janitor to paid disco coach, Matteo saves his money from working at Arthur Murray's. Before the summer is out, he proposes to Kristin, and she accepts. When the two set the date, their respective families disown them, Matteo's for choosing to marry a non-Italian Protestant, and Kristin's for choosing to marry an Italian Catholic. Why don't we get hitched out of state, says Matteo? There's a disco in DC I always wanted to go to. What about Studio 54? asks Kristin. We never did get there. No thanks, says Matteo. That was the past.

The pair drive to New Jersey and then take a train to the nation's capital. When they arrive, they discover that they have a choice: spend all the money they have left on getting married, or splurge at the disco, whose cover charge is more than either had ever imagined. Disco's for kids who don't want to grow up, says Matteo, counting his cash for the fifth time. Are you sure? asks Kristin. Because the last thing I want to have to compete with is dance. With you, it might win.

The Honeymoon

Husband and wife spend their honeymoon on the next train back to New Jersey, alternating between making love standing up in a one-person lavatory and talking. Kristin finds out that Matteo is good at fixing just about anything that gets broken, and Matteo finds out that Kristin doesn't know how to cook. Then I won't get fat, he says. I don't mind eating frozen dinners, as long as the meals are calm and don't involve arguing. You heard my parents. Kristin nods. As long as we don't end up giving each other the silent treatment, she says. My parents are pros at that. Both agree that they'll live a life that's neither Catholic nor Protestant, neither Italian nor Anglo. What about children? asks Matteo. We don't need any of those, either, says Kristin. It'll just be us.

The First Month of Marriage

Back home, the newlyweds move into an apartment above the Arthur Murray Dance Studio. Kristin gets a job as a waitress, while Matteo quits coaching dance to work five days at a real estate agency and four nights in a factory. Both postpone college. Unable to afford heat, they use the gas burners in the kitchen. See the blue flame? says Matteo, huddled by the stove with his wife on a winter night. Imagine it's a disco light, you know, one of those pole thingies flashing on and off at Studio 54. Is that what it is? says Kristin. You sound like you've been there. I have, says Matteo, with you in my dreams. During the coldest part of the winter, Matteo and Kristin stand before the stove and dance the hustle, YMCA, and a lot of freestyle disco. In bed, they warm up with sex, during which Kristin holds her breath to keep from making sounds that might disturb her husband.

The Memento

Oftentimes, especially in old cheesy movies, a jealous wife or girlfriend finds a memento—lipstick-stained handkerchief, phone number scrawled on the back of a book of matches, take your pick—which she uses as evidence to expose and break up a triangle. In the case of Kristin, Matteo, and Nina, no such scenario transpires, despite the fact that Matteo not only saves Nina's broken, five-inch heel, but also keeps it after he marries Kristin. The wooden heel, which both he and Nina forgot about after the trip to Studio 54, is still in his jacket pocket, that is, until his second month of marriage, when he ends up using it to jury-rig a frying pan, whose handle breaks and causes Kristin to get a second-degree burn while she's trying to make scrambled eggs. After unscrewing the broken handle, Matteo drills a hole in the middle of the high heel and attaches it to the pan with a long bolt. You are so talented and creative, says Kristin, lying in bed, looking at Matteo's master design, as he scoops a fluffy omelet from pan to plate. Kristin reaches with her right hand for a fork. Oh, no you don't, says Matteo. I don't want you to use that hand for one second, not until the burn is fully healed. I will feed you. Kristin says the panhandle looks like the heel of a woman's shoe, and Matteo says she's right. Where did you get it? she asks. Stole it from a woman I took to Studio 54 before we were married, he says. Right on, says Kristin. I believe it. Serious Catholic boy afraid to kiss me on our first date: he stole it, ripped it off a woman's shoe, dancing at Studio 54.

The Inheritance

As spring approaches, Matteo finds he has inherited a farmhouse outside Pocono Pinnacle, as well as a healthy sum of money from his father's bachelor brother. Uncle Gug, whom Matteo had only met once, changed his will shortly after Matteo's father disowned his only son. The newlyweds move into the farmhouse and use a chunk of the inheritance to finish college, both working full time while studying business. Neither has the inclination or time to dance disco.

A Dance for Three

One might think that the friendship between Nina and Kristin couldn't possibly survive once Kristin marries Matteo and settles into the farmhouse because triangles never work and three's a crowd. Not so fast. We mustn't forget what is known in the professional dance world as a *pas de trois,* or dance for three. For Kristin, Matteo, and Nina, such a dance causes a friendship to blossom and a misunderstanding to blow over, at least for a while. However, the scenario leading up to this cozy little dance is nothing other than tragic.

When Nina's parents are stabbed to death by the antlers of a deer that crashes through the windshield of their car, Kristin visits Nina every night for a week to see if she's all right. I can't stand it living here, says Nina. Then come stay with us, says Kristin. You know that little guesthouse behind the garage? It's yours for as long as you need it. No thanks, says Nina. You need your privacy. Kristin says the guesthouse is set up with a full kitchen, bed, and bath. Don't you need to consult Matteo first? asks Nina. Not when it comes to my best friend, says Kristin. We're family.

At first, Nina and Matteo barely exchange hellos, before Nina isolates herself in the guesthouse. Her depression worsens. I keep seeing that animal, says Nina over an evening cup of tea with Kristin. That deer was so graceful when I first saw it—like a ballet dancer leaping across the road. Then, a second later, all the blood. Kristin puts her arms around Nina. Think about how your father still managed to stop the car before he died, says Kristin. You're alive, and you've got friends who care very much about you.

I don't think being here is doing her any good, says Matteo, a week after Nina's arrival. Give it a chance, says Kristin. Maybe if you were a little more sociable, she might feel more welcome.

On an unseasonably warm Friday evening in May, Kristin gets the idea to ask Nina for a cooking lesson. I know your mother made wonderful marinara sauce, says Kristin. Teach me how to make it. At first Nina says no, but Kristin persists. When the two have gathered the ingredients, Nina begins to come around. You have to be very careful to remove all of the center vein, says Nina, slicing into a clove of garlic. Otherwise, the sauce breeds indigestion. Kristin writes down Nina's tips, while Nina looks for a saucepan to sauté the onions and garlic in extra virgin olive oil. This is when she finds the pan with her old disco heel for a handle. Oh my God, she says. I don't believe it. Kristin lets out a laugh. Oh, that, she says. It's exactly what it looks like: the broken heel of a ladies' pump. One of Matteo's crafty projects, borne out of poverty and a desire to keep me from getting burned. Now it serves as a memento of how poor we once were. Nina asks Kristin where the heel came from, and Kristin says, who knows? Matteo's always collecting stuff from dumpsters and all sorts of places. That's what happens when you marry a janitor.

When Matteo tries Kristin's marinara atop homemade mostaccioli, he says is the best he's ever tasted, and the three reminisce about their high school days. They get drunk on Fernet-Branca, an Italian liqueur Nina's parents had purchased in Philadelphia. None of the three have ever tasted the bitter, after-dinner drink. No one really knows what goes into the liqueur, says Nina, but sources say that the ingredients come from three continents. Matteo challenges the two to shimmy, while saying, sources say, no one knows, five times fast. Nina takes the challenge and ends up coughing from laughing so much. Kristin puts on a record of The Village People, and the three perform YMCA, laughing as they attempt to form the four letters of the abbreviation for which the dance is named. When the song ends, Kristin starts it over and whispers in Nina's ear, telling her to stand next to Matteo and do the bump when forming the C. Both Nina and Kristin knock Matteo off balance, and he reacts by grabbing their arms. All three land on the floor,

Matteo on the bottom, Kristin in the middle, and Nina on top. Matteo wriggles out, while Nina sits firmly on Kristin's hips, looking at Matteo.

The Confession

Six months later, well after Nina has moved back into her parents' home, fixed it up, and turned it into a bed and breakfast, Matteo gets cancer and lands in the hospital. Kristin visits him every day after work, while Nina prepares dinner for her best friend. On his deathbed, Matteo confesses to Kristin that he slept with Nina, just one time, he says, in New York, after my one and only visit to Studio 54. How was it? asks Kristin, her voice calm and low. I would have rather gone with you, says Matteo. Kristin folds her arms and presses them against her ribs. I'm talking about the sex, you idiot, not Studio 54. It was horrible, says Matteo, worse than the fucking heart monitor beeping in my ears. Oh, says Kristin. A real squealer. What can I say? says Matteo. Kristin unfolds her arms and stands up. Just tell me this: what was it like dancing with Nina at Studio 54? Matteo begins to cough, and Kristin hands him a cup of water. He takes a drink and stops coughing. I want to know the truth, she says. Matteo clears his throat. Dancing with that woman at Studio 54 will land me in hell. Kristin flashes a smirk. That good, was it? Matteo nods and tells Kristin about the disco heel. It was crazy, he says. I looked all over for something to replace that panhandle, and the disco heel was all I could come up with. Kristin asks why he never told her the truth about Nina. I don't know, says Matteo. Guess I was a coward. But having that damn pan with a heel stuck in it served as a reminder I'd have to tell you some time. Don't worry about it, says Kristin. I may be straight-laced, but I'm not my parents.

The Wake, Part I

Just as Patrizia von Brandenstein went shopping at a Brooklyn clothing store to find what would become John Travolta's iconic white suit in *Saturday Night Fever,* Kristin goes to Scranton to buy a similar outfit for Matteo's wake—white jacket and pants, black shirt, and white vest. A friend who's a mortician prepares the

152

body and brings it to the farmhouse. Lying in the John Travolta suit in a glossy white casket with burgundy velvet padding, what's left of Matteo is on display for friends from work, high school, and college to pay their respects. Obstructing his wavy black hair, some of which had fallen out during treatments, is a pair of fluffy brown earmuffs. These are the ones he used to wear when mowing the lawn to block out the noise, says Kristin. I put them on him because they represent Matteo's quirkiness. Loving him was not easy. In the middle of our second date, he asked me if I'd be willing to cut my fingernails short. That was so I didn't make the clicking sound he couldn't stand. I said yes. Sometimes I think that *yes* was more important than the one I gave when he asked me to marry him. Maybe I wasn't the most exciting person, but we still ended up together, and I'm glad. I just wish it could have been for longer.

Travolta

There's a classic moment in *Saturday Night Fever,* when John Travolta performs a solo to the Bee Gees' most famous tune: *Stayin' Alive.* Colored lights flashing and disco ball rolling, Travolta lunges back with his left leg. The moment we hear, *Life goin' nowhere. Somebody help me,* Travolta folds out his right arm and pivots his torso to point at his audience, gathered on all sides along the flanks of the dance floor.

The Wake, Part II

After people applaud Kristin's speech, she puts a Bee Gees record on the stereo. About three minutes into *Stayin' Alive,* she imitates the aforementioned move, finishing it off by pointing at Nina. Everyone except Nina applauds, and Kristin takes a curtsy. I was never good enough to accompany Matteo to a real disco, she says. Oh no, says Joe, Nina's ex-boyfriend who dumped her for a cheerleader when they were in high school. I thought you were great. Keep dancing. No thanks, says Kristin, but maybe someone else will. Nina, why don't you show us how you do the hustle. You're so good at it. I've got the music right here. Nina declines, but Kristin presses on. Matteo would have wanted you to, she says. I've got a terrible headache, says Nina, excusing herself to go to the bathroom, where she stays until their friends and former classmates leave the house. When she comes out, Kristin asks her to help her clean up in the kitchen.

I Will Survive

Sitting on the top burner of the stove is the frying pan with Nina's old high heel for a handle. You wash, and I'll dry, says Kristin, opening the drawer and taking out a dish towel featuring a picture of Olivia Newton John from the film *Xanadu*. We need to talk, says Nina. Sure, says Kristin, but you wash, and I'll dry, unless you want me to do the washing. Can't we just talk first, says Nina? Can't the cleanup wait? Kristin drops the frying pan on the floor, and the heel falls off. She lets out a guffaw. It's about time that thing came apart, she says. All part of the cleanup. Nina starts to say something, and Kristin excuses herself to put on some music. Just as Gloria Gaynor sings, *I will survive,* Kristin returns. You're not washing, she says, grabbing the dishwashing liquid and squirting it in the air so light blue bubbles go floating past Nina's nose. Almost like being at Studio 54, says Kristin, performing a shadow turn. I hear they have colored lights that look like bubbles. Enough, says Nina. I get your point.

The women face the kitchen sink, looking out the window onto the steely November sky, dead stalks of San Marzano tomato plants waving back and forth in Matteo's garden. Gaynor continues to sing. Suddenly, the stereo lets out a high-pitched shriek, followed by a slowed distortion of Gaynor's voice: *I've been spending nights thinking how you did me wrooooong.* The record is scratched, says Kristin. I need to turn it off.

The Dance Quiz

Directions, Part I: Take off your clothes and read each question carefully while sitting before a floor-length mirror. Then choose what you believe is the correct answer. When you circle your answer, feel how your body adjusts to the movement. Enjoy the dance.

Question 1: A 30-something woman with marital problems and a fit body decides to take a day hike through a remote part of Yosemite National Park. Whom should she choose as her male hiking partner in order to have a safe, productive hike with conversation that inspires her to address her problems with aplomb?

a. the hardcore bodybuilder from the gym, who has asked her out before, but to no avail

b. her uncle, who served as a medic in Iraq

c. the minister from her church, who has taken Boy Scouts on camping trips in various parts of the park

d. a gay Facebook friend from her childhood, who quit his career as a professional ballet dancer to study psychology

If you chose **a**,

you want the woman to get it on with the hot bodybuilder, so she can free herself from an unhappy marriage, first in her mind and then on paper in Las Vegas. You want the woman and the bodybuilder to spread a blanket by a remote waterfall and let nature take over. Whether you're male or female, gay or straight, you want to watch, feel their bodies indulging in the sinew of each other's adrenaline, the release of inhibitions in the midst of the wilderness. You are a voyeur. You are the sort who would follow at a distance, wait behind a bush, watch the lovers dig their bodies into the sand, as the waterfall sprays mist onto their glistening skin.

The image is definitely a hot one, but it has clouded your

judgment. You have failed to take into account the bodybuilder's inability to converse productively about much other than bodybuilding, sports supplements, and sex. As much as the woman may want to succumb to libidinal yearning, she upholds standards, which is why she was attracted to her husband and not some vacuous jock in the first place. Yet both her husband and the bodybuilder have a similar way of pronouncing their a's—her husband when discussing his research of Albanian art history and the bodybuilder when talking about the use of anabolic steroids. Furthermore, the bodybuilder has come to her aid a number of times, when she has needed a spot for the Smith machine. He's definitely someone to have around in a pinch. However, the man is far from the right choice for a hiking partner, not for this hike, not when the woman needs a good listener, someone to think about what she says, someone intellectually capable of responding to her thoughts about her husband's obsession with The Dancing Snake, an ancient Albanian sculpture recently excavated and highly prized by museums across the world.

If you chose **b**,
you're thinking logically, since the woman's uncle has the knowledge and ability to apply multiple forms of first aid, should the hikers encounter unexpected dangers. He has always been a family man, who took care of his wife during her remission from breast cancer and believes that couples need to work hard to make their marriages succeed. The woman's uncle has always been fond of his niece, whom he nicknamed Riki-tikki-tavi, when, as a little girl staying the night with her cousins, she heard a noise in the attic and went up to investigate. Instead of screaming when she saw a snake, she found an empty shoebox and trapped it for further observation. The woman has never liked her nickname and has told her uncle many a time that "Rudyard Kipling's Rikki-tikki-tavi was a mongoose that killed cobras, not a girl with a curiosity for nature." How much the woman will confide in her uncle because of this incident is unknown, but rest assured that her uncle possesses few inhibitions when expressing his opinion. Such an attitude

worked well with his wife's doctors; however, his niece is not looking for someone to solve her problems. She will definitely react negatively, if her uncle tries to give advice. While the big, lumbering man might be good to have around if a rabid bear comes along and tries to attack the two on their hike, since he always carries a .38 and holds a record for his quick draw, he is definitely not the right choice.

If you chose **c**,

your big mistake is assuming that the minister, because of his profession, is morally worthy of accompanying the woman through the woods. Nowhere in Question 1 did I give you any information about his ethical aptitude. You have mistakenly relied on stereotypes—a sign of backward and lazy thinking, that, in its nature, promotes discrimination. And now, the moment I turn my back, you're doing it again. Stop thinking of the minister as a rapist or child molester. Quit acting like an idiot for God's sake. What disqualifies the man of the cloth is his own obsession with his vocation—not the ministry, but the little business he has on the side: the good reverend catches poisonous snakes and sells them to ministers from snake-handling churches from across the land. Although he does not believe in the literal translation of Mark 16: 17-18, he does provide the means for ministers to "take up serpents," a violation of U.S. law in all states except West Virginia, of which he is not a resident. For him the hike would serve as a scouting trip, minus the boys. An expert in finding Western diamondback rattlers, he would take note of any signs of the creatures and then come back to trap them on his own.

Considering that the woman is an animal rights activist and lover of snakes, she would be more than distressed if she ever found out that she inadvertently contributed to the future abuse of snakes. Furthermore, she is quite aware that the abuse does not stop with the animals. She knows that snake handlers confine copperheads and rattlers to wooden boxes, often placed beneath their children's beds to get them used to the sound of hissing, before brandishing their "serpents" in church. She does not believe that Americans' freedom of religion applies to a sect of Christianity that requires "true believers" to expose themselves to wild and abused reptiles and refuse to seek medical attention when bitten.

However, the fact that the woman's husband is obsessed with a sculpture of a snake might make for interesting conversation with the minister, who has a degree in herpetology. Also, the woman might discover that the minister is more interested in looking for snake dens than talking to her, and may become suspicious. Perhaps she could even help apprehend the minister in the future. But such is not her goal, which I define quite clearly in the text of the question. Therefore, c is most definitely the wrong answer.

If you chose **d**,

Woohoo: you got it right. The ex-ballet dancer studying psychology is the best candidate for four important reasons: he's a good listener, he knows what it means to dedicate himself to details, he has no agenda beyond friendship with the woman, and he knows how to partner a woman when performing a *grand jeté*.

Question 2: How could the gay dancer's ability to perform a fancy leap while lifting his partner benefit the woman, as the two hike through the mountains?

　　a. As the woman and man dance in the wilderness, the woman remembers a time in her youth when she studied ballet, when she was interested in a career as a dancer, not a career as a wife with a job on the side.

　　b. The gay dancer's moves, coupled with his current pursuit of a career in psychology, cause the woman to relate her husband's obsession with a snake sculpture to latent homosexual tendencies he may harbor in his subconscious.

　　c. The fact that the woman can act spontaneously when the dancer reveals his intention to lift her in a *grand jeté* causes her to reflect on the lack of spontaneity in her sex life with her husband.

d. The man saves the woman's life, as well as his own, by orchestrating a supported *grand jeté.*

e. All of the above are true.

If you **forsook a,**

picture the two on a flat section of the Panorama Trail overlooking a foreground of tall, thin, and dark conifers set far apart in a landscape of steely peaks, curved and conical. Masculine and feminine blur into one, as they perform their dance. Seeing them leap across the trail, forming their own mountains as they arc upward, makes you want to perform your own *grand jeté,* even if you harbor the deep-seated suspicion that the scene celebrates sentimentality. You have never felt so free when you become the woman, when you feel the man— his hands powerful, his touch elegant—lift you high into the air, as if you are competing with the peaks. When the woman says, "I used to love to jump," you share in her childhood memory, reliving your own experience of propelling your body against gravity, shouting with excitement, relishing independence.

Then, while hanging your head, out of breath from performing an act that reminds you of your physical limitations, you recognize the sophistication of children at play, of dancers executing technique that on one hand preserves a strict distinction between genders, and on the other, allows humans to experience unprecedented freedom from commonality, mediocrity. You don't think about imagining perfection—a perfect career, a perfect body, a perfect sense of self. Instead, you feel it. You feel what the woman feels—loss of childhood ideals somehow regained through body memory.

Unfortunately, you forsook letter a, which means you did not allow yourself the chance to indulge in any of these experiences or feelings. You failed to exercise both your body and your imagination. Unlike the woman, you will not see hope in the future. You will do nothing about your life and will continue to think and move as you always have.

If you **forsook b,**

perhaps you dreaded the hiking couple's discussion of Freud's essay "The Uncanny," how the unfamiliar can induce dread and horror. You were not in the least bit interested in the image of the woman recoiling when the man likened her husband's obsession with the snake sculpture to the possibility that the work of art serves as an opaque and clichéd mask for the husband's desire for man-to-man sexual gratification. You hate the idea of being induced to look for symbols and imagery in everyday life and never thought much of the study of literature. Yet if you were there on the trail, you wouldn't be able to hide your excitement when the dancer who studies psychology performs a series of movements, in which his body becomes a phallus, pulsating with liquid repetition. You feel for the woman, who laughs at the dancer's movements while adjusting her socks, which have fallen below her ankle bones. When the dancer says, "I'm not sure if I can make it through college," after he is through with his performance, you feel for him as well. You wish that each will say to the other, "I'll help you through it," but neither says anything. They just keep hiking, each captivated by his or her own "creeping horror."

If you **forsook c,**

you're stuck in a rut formed by Lewis and Clark, wagon wheels, and westward expansion. You relate well to the woman's uncle and his desire to make the world right with guns and phallic hegemony, while hiding the tenderness he expressed when his wife was sick. You see the dancer's speech and actions as irrelevant when he grabs her right armpit with his left hand and her right hand with his right hand and tells her to *grand jeté*. You think they are just fooling around, hiding from reality, acting like silly children. You don't even notice the synchronized action of their leap—front legs developing from bent to straight, bodies grazing the atmosphere. You have no idea how such spontaneity, induced by a gay ballet dancer with sinewy legs and buttocks, causes the woman to reflect upon the steps—safe, precise, and uniform—she has taken for four years of marriage to ensure that the man she is married to achieves an orgasm after a sleepy hour's stint. You see none of this. In other words, you can't dance.

If you **forsook d,**
you failed to see the snake—the Western diamondback rattler coiled up in the middle of the trail as the pair walked briskly, paying more attention to the sculpted mountains than the earth below. You allowed the brown markings of the snake to blend in with the variegated stone and soil upon which the serpent lay basking, asleep in the sun. You failed to acknowledge the power of subtlety—the snake's, the dancer's, and the woman's. You automatically assumed that such a so-called feminine trait as subtlety was somehow unworthy of your attention. If it had been you walking by, you most definitely would have been bitten. The gun in your pocket would have done no good once the venom was flowing in your bloodstream. The moment of satisfaction you would have achieved from shooting the snake would have been short-lived. You, unlike the man and woman, would never have the pleasure to argue with another man farther down the trail, a ranger who denied the fact that humans could outmaneuver a snake, whose reaction time was "at least ten times faster than an Olympiad." You wouldn't be there to watch the dancer and woman snicker at the ranger's reference to sports, his inability to acknowledge the power of dance.

If you **chose e,**
you are correct. Life is complex. Sometimes you need to experience negativity in order to live.

Question 3: What happens to the woman after the hike?
a. She introduces the ex-dancer to her husband, who falls asleep while the ex-dancer talks. The ex-dancer changes his mind about the husband's sexual orientation.
b. She invites the minister and her uncle to dinner. Both show an interest in the husband's research, and the woman ends up feeling left out of the conversation, until she finds out that The Dancing Snake sculpture was a fertility icon worshipped by pagan Albanians.
c. She confronts her husband about his lack of attention,

and he tells her he's becoming impotent.

d. She takes an interest in her husband's research, but his behavior fails to change. Learning the lurid details of The Dancing Snake's influence on pagan Albanians, she proceeds to have an affair with the bodybuilder, who ends up giving her a sexually transmitted infection.

e. She hires a private investigator to follow her husband and finds out he is spending his time studying The Dancing Snake, alongside the pagan rituals associated with the sculpture. When she attempts to adapt some of those rituals in the bedroom with her husband, she finds out he is impotent and tells him it's all right.

f. She introduces the bodybuilder to her husband, who falls asleep while the bodybuilder talks. Then she enrolls in adult ballet classes five nights a week.

g. She arranges to meet with the minister, who fails to show up because he has been arrested for harboring snakes illegally.

h. She enrolls in ballet classes for five nights a week. After a month of dancing, she confronts her husband, who tells her he is in love with The Dancing Snake.

i. You decide what happens, based on a combination of possibilities listed in a through h.

If you chose **a** or **b** or **c** or **d** or **e** or **f** or **g** or **h** or **i**, you may receive full credit for your answer, as long as you can demonstrate in a 500-word typed essay, to be attached to this document, how the woman was influenced by dance as the story unfolds. Of course you will need to define "dance" in order to provide a logical argument based on substantiated claims.

Directions, Part II: Put some clothes on—tights then leotards and ballet slippers for women; dance belt, leotards, tights, waist belt, and ballet slippers for men. Look at yourself in a floor-to-ceiling mirror. Go online and look up images of ballet dancers in practice wear. Compare yourself to those images. Reread this document alongside your answers while executing a *grand plié* in fifth position. If you do not know how to perform a grand plié, go onto YouTube and find an example of a professional dancer from a world-class company performing a series of *pliés*. To the best of your ability, imitate what you see. Then answer the following questions.

Question 4: Based on your interpretation of the story of the woman with marital problems who dances with the former ballet dancer in order to avoid the wrath of a poisonous snake, why do you think ballet attracts a good number of gay men?

    a. Ballet *is* gay.

    b. Who else but a gay man would wear clothes that show off his genitalia and buttocks?

    c. Gay men are an abomination against the Father, Son, and Holy Spirit because they ignore the Bible.

    d. Gay men often take better care of their bodies and are more able to balance feminine and masculine traits inherent in all humans; therefore, they have the capacity to become superior ballet dancers, since ballet requires a sense of harmony between masculine and feminine traits.

If you chose **a**,

you think you're straight, and you went to an American high school between 2010-2018. You consider it cool to use the term *gay* to refer to anything the cool kids dislike. You have no idea that discrimination against gay men is a form of misogyny, and your reading comprehension skills reflect an all-time low in American educational history. You don't get the fact that a "big, lumbering man" might not be the best choice to have around when treading through snake country. You fail to take note that the steps the dancer and woman took before they leapt over the snake were light enough to ensure that the sleeping serpent failed to wake up. Instead, if you bothered to read at all, you praise the uncle for his ability to shoot and kill. Never would you challenge his masculinity, and if you were put in the same situation, you would take the straight and narrow, follow in the uncle's footsteps, step right on top of the snake.

If you chose **b**,

you wear long, baggy shorts as an excuse for a swimsuit if you're a man. You expect "real men" to wear long, baggy shorts that you consider "normal" for a swimsuit, if you're a woman. You fail to take into account that these so-called "real men" hide their male anatomy in the process of adhering to a code of masculinity. You fail to consider the possibility that so-called masculine men are afraid to break that code, that these "masculine men" are afraid of their own anatomy. Considering the fact that the expression of emotions, particularly fear, breaks the masculine code, you fail to acknowledge the hypocrisy of men in baggy shorts. Instead, you work hard to be a good little obedient follower, laughing at men in tights, men who express emotion on stage, men who are in touch with the anatomy and physiology of their bodies, men who respect women. In other words, you fail to realize that gay or straight, male ballet dancers who lift women high into the air and touch their bodies with sensitivity and lyricism, are the real men of the world, not a bunch of Neanderthals jumping atop each other's buttocks on a football field and calling it a tackle. The gay ex-ballet dancer who saved the woman from the snake is a lot more man than you will ever know.

If you chose **c**,

you are a Christian hypocrite, especially if you don't believe in handling snakes in church. You pick and choose parts of the Bible that you interpret as you are told, failing to take into account that literal interpretations of this text, especially Mark 16: 17-18, often result in death and destruction: *And these signs shall follow them that believe; In my name shall they cast out devils; they shall speak with new tongues; They shall take up serpents; and if they drink any deadly thing, it shall not hurt them; they shall lay hands on the sick, and they shall recover.* You are like the woman's minister, preaching what he considers the Word of God on Sundays, quoting animal lover Francis of Assisi, and then trapping and selling poisonous snakes for personal profit. Your hypocrisy is validated when you read Mark 16: 17-18 and know better than to interpret the words literally, and then read Leviticus 20:13 and interpret the passage word for word: "If a man has sexual relations with a man as one does with a woman, both of them have done what is detestable. They will be put to death; their blood will be on their own heads." Finally, you have a problem with logic, for men couldn't possibly have sex with other men exactly the way men have sex with women. Men are built differently.

If you chose **d**,
I shouldn't have to tell you if you are correct or not. This is not about being correct. It's about assumptions and stereotypes and seeking truth. It's about asking questions, not filling out a test and reading a story. You know that the woman, the woman's husband, the bodybuilder, the uncle, the minister, and the ex-dancer aren't real. Or are they? Is your view of these fictional characters a reality that will determine how you treat others, especially those not like you? You want to hear me say that your answer is correct, so you can seek validation and then forget about people. I won't.

Question 5: If the woman, the woman's husband, the bodybuilder, the uncle, the minister, and the ex-dancer are all placed in the same locked room with the prompt that they cannot leave until each one expresses her or his greatest vulnerability, what would happen?
    a. The uncle and bodybuilder would join forces to find a way out of the room without considering the prompt.
    b. The woman and ex-dancer would perform a *pas de deux*.
    c. The minister would lead the group in a prayer.
    d. The woman's husband would speak of his obsession with the past, alongside his inability to get close to anyone in the present.
    e. All of the above are true.
    f. None of the above is true.
    g. The previous two answers are equally true.
    h. Truth is a dance we perform when negotiating our way through culture. That dance is made up of plies, words, *grand jetés,* facial expressions, and silence.

Again, you decide what the right answer is. And when you're done, think about the harshness you harbor—the severity of what you *don't* say, the acidity of what you *think* and *believe*. Did you ever stop to wonder why ballet is so esoteric, while football is admired by people from all walks of life? Perhaps the answer is in the fact that ballet fails to assume the reputation of a violent sport, in which opponents crush the competition while spectators shout with excitement.

The Continental

Beautiful music ... Dangerous rhythm ...

It's something daring, The Continental, a way of dancing that's really "entre nous."

It's very subtle, The Continental, because it does what you want it to do.

—Con Conrad, music

—Herb Magidson, lyrics

Introduced by Fred Astaire and Ginger Rogers in the 1934 film *The Gay Divorcé,* The Continental caught on quickly. Glued to their Philco radios, the hippest of hepcats sang along. Someone's idea to feature twenty-seven step-by-step photos of America's dancing sweethearts performing The Continental did wonders when it came to selling sheet music. However, the dance itself did not fare so well. It was too hard, its performers too good. Millie, a teen from Massachusetts, used to study the photos and imitate Rogers while humming the tune. She even went out with a ballroom dance instructor, who taught her the first section of The Continental. But once she married Harmon, she lost interest in the dance, that is, until 2012, when she became ill.

* * *

Millie dips her fork in the soup and swirls it around, as if she's gathering spaghetti. Coming up empty, she gazes at Harmon, her eyes sinking into the wrinkles in her cheeks.

Harmon hands her a spoon. "Try this."

He worries that his words sound sarcastic, that some part of Millie will take offense.

Millie drops the utensil—plink—into the soup.

Letting out a sigh, Harmon retrieves the spoon, wipes it off, and urges his wife to eat.

Millie begins to dance in her seat, feet shuffling on the floor, shoulders bouncing to a beat in her head. "Hash browns! My hash browns!"

Betty Lynn waves to Millie, as she takes an order on the opposite side of the diner. "Be right with you, Hon."

Harmon reaches across the table and rubs his wife's shoulders. When she stops dancing, he hands her the spoon. She eats.

When the hash browns arrive, Millie pokes them with her fork. As usual, they land on the floor. Betty Lynn picks up the food. She doesn't charge them for what's fallen. She never does. Harmon gives her a thirty-percent tip, and the waitress escorts the couple to their car.

"See you tomorrow," says Betty Lynn.

"You bet," says Harmon.

Millie waves.

Millie and Harmon have eaten at the diner for seventeen years. Neither have cholesterol or heart problems, but they watch their diets, which isn't easy to do at a place called The Grease in the Pan. Chosen because of its name, the restaurant has become a way of life for the couple, especially during Millie's illness.

"Intriguing and refreshingly frank," she had said, when they first drove by. "Only in the South."

On their first visit to the restaurant, they were greeted by a long map of the Appalachian Trail, along with a list of names of locals who had hiked the seventy-five miles it ambles through the state of Georgia. By the summer of their second year of retirement, their names were on the list. When their granddaughter Brianna came to stay, they took her to The Grease in the Pan. Brianna ordered hash browns, which she couldn't finish, and Millie asked for a box. When Harmon hit a bump in the road, the potatoes popped out of the Styrofoam and slid under the passenger seat.

"My hash browns!" cried Brianna." My hash browns!"

Millie consoled Brianna, Harmon cleaned the grease stains, and the matter was dropped. The brain is a strange being, Harmon has begun to realize. Even in the midst of disease, it clings to the oddest things. Millie and Brianna have the same pug nose.

Last fall, when Harmon and Millie drove up to Massachusetts, Millie mistook Brianna for Julie, their daughter. Twice she told Harmon to hurry up, or she would be late for her dance lesson. In February, when Julie and Brianna stopped in on their way to Sarasota, Millie failed to recognize either one. Of course Julie overreacted and never made it to Florida. Instead, she made a nuisance at the doctor's, cooked enough food to last a month, and cried on her father's shoulder. Harmon wishes she would get remarried.

* * *

When not attending to his wife, Harmon spends a good deal of time on the internet. He's a member of an Alzheimer's online support group and sells old-time radio parts on eBay. At 82, he drives and doesn't need glasses. At five-foot-seven, he still has a thirty-inch waist. Every afternoon he takes a half-mile walk while Millie sleeps. Wearing his pedometer, he goes from the living room to the kitchen to the bedrooms and back— 360 times. Before Millie got sick, the two had hiked the North Georgia foothills at least once a week. During his indoor walks, Harmon thinks of ways to make his wife happy. The doctors don't know how much longer she'll be able to recognize him, and he wants to make the best of it. Lately, he's been playing old records. Sometimes, when the birds are singing, Millie wants the music turned off. Some songs she hates one day and then loves the next. Last Tuesday, she called Bing Crosby "the Devil." On Wednesday, she listened to *White Christmas* thirty-two times. Harmon has worn a path in the carpet during his walks.

If Millie's awake and the phone rings, Harmon encourages her to answer. As long as his wife knows how to say, "Hello," he's satisfied. Her voice sounds like that of a little girl with laryngitis—a child who knows how to scream with delight as she rides down the slide, not an octogenarian who smoked for a decade before giving birth. She can still say the phrase *fine, thank you,* and takes great pleasure in doing it. Harmon is convinced that as long as she stays happy, her condition deteriorates at a slower pace. Since they got on the no-call list, the phone has

169

been mostly silent. Millie's sister used to call from Tallahassee, but now she's got Alzheimer's, too.

Halfway into Harmon's walk, the phone rings. He picks up the extension just as Millie answers. The line is silent, except for a sigh followed by a loud swallow. He knows who it is, even without Caller ID.

"Julie," says Harmon. "What's wrong?"

His daughter sighs again. "I've got a mother whose brain is mush and a father who knows who you are and how you feel by the way you breathe."

"Ever since you didn't get first prize in the cake competition, I've been listening to that sigh," says Harmon. "You were 17. Now tell me, what's going on?"

Julie hisses. "Don't forget a thing, do you?"

Harmon smiles. "Sure I do. I can't remember the last time you used a civil tongue when talking to your father."

"Why do you let Mom answer the phone?"

"And why do you let Brianna watch television?—just as silly a question. Now come on. I don't want to argue with you. I know that something's up, and I can't help you, if you won't tell me what it is."

Harmon and Julie hear a crash.

"What was that?" says Julie.

"I need to check on your mother."

"Wait!" Julie's voice goes up an octave. "What's happening?"

"Julie, calm down."

"Has Mom become violent?"

"No, she has not. Talk to you later."

* * *

Ever since her husband died, Julie has become paranoid of losing Brianna. If the school bus is late, she calls the police. If the child sneezes, she rushes her to the doctor. Almost a year ago, it took nearly a week of phone calls and emails to convince Julie not to take Brianna out of school, after the poor girl twisted her ankle during recess. Harmon has nicknamed Julie "the vicarious hypochondriac." Now that she's in counseling, things are a bit better. He'll call her later.

Neither he nor Millie spanked or hit Julie when she was growing up. They rarely argued, and always did so with low voices, whether Julie was around or not. The only time Harmon ever got violent was in the middle of a nightmare. It was one of those dreams that rattle the skin, that make you feel as if your organs have somehow gone inside out. The car had run out of gas. As he and Millie and Julie walked down a steep hill toward the nearest station, the parking brake came loose, and the car came at them. Husband shoved wife and child into a ditch. In real life, Harmon knocked Millie out of bed. When he explained the dream, Millie said she understood, but he knew she was shaken. He went out and bought a bigger bed. They made love in it the day it arrived. When the payments became a burden, Millie took on a summer secretarial job. They both slept well in the king-size bed, which they gave to Julie, when they left for the mountains of Georgia.

Harmon finds Millie sitting on the guest bedroom floor, swaying back and forth, holding one of Julie's old wooden blocks. The phone receiver dangles. Millie's hair, a combination of gray and white waves, accentuates the lack of expression on her face. Harmon puts back the receiver and sits on the floor. The blocks are stacked in a way that reminds him of the coastal New England saltbox where Millie was born.

"Nantasket," says Harmon, referring to their hometown.

"Nan-tas-ket," says Millie, brushing her hair behind her ears. For a moment, her expression transforms from stiff and wooden to soft and sinuous, like the oxbow of the brook in her parents' front yard, where as a boy, Harmon had accidentally tossed a newspaper. Her lips part, as if she's about to say something, and when she can't, her face regains its rigor mortis. Harmon uses a tissue to wipe away the drool.

"I don't know," says Millie. "I don't know."

Harmon holds her tightly.

* * *

Betty Lynn meets Harmon and Millie in the parking lot of

171

The Grease in the Pan. She tells Harmon that the owner wants to use Millie's picture on the restaurant's Web site. "The one of Millie and Brianna standing at the salad bar."

Harmon says he'll think about it. When Millie's hash browns land on the shoes of an out-of-town customer, Harmon apologizes. After the meal, he agrees to the photo and offers Betty Lynn an extra $5. She hands it back.

"You don't need to worry," she says. "Y'all are family. Should know that by now."

* * *

Harmon and Millie own a house in a development built in the '80s. They live on a steep and rutted dirt path that's supposed to be maintained by the residents. One of the neighbors refuses to contribute his share, so neither does anyone else. Every spring the ruts and potholes get bigger. Last winter, when nine inches of snow stranded residents for a week, Betty Lynn came in an ATV filled with supplies. When she found out that Millie had a cold, she stayed long enough to make a pot of soup beans with ham.

Soup is one of the words Millie remembers, along with *corn* and *farm*.

Whenever they're driving, and Millie sees rows of corn growing along the hillsides, she leans out the window and sings, "Farm-farm-farm, corn farm," bobbing her head from side to side.

"Harmon says, "Yes," and repeats his wife's phrase.

Harmon loves to drive but goes only as far as Millie allows. Even though she can't say much, he knows when she's had enough. There's a noise she makes. A cross between a sigh and a bleat, the warning signal can come at any time, even after Millie has gleefully identified every patch of corn between The Grease in the Pan and the North Carolina border. When he first heard the sound, Harmon wasn't sure if Millie were content or in distress. The exhalation appeared cathartic, while the bleat reminded him of a fawn demanding milk from its mother. Still unsure of how to interpret the expression, Harmon sees it as a

172

sign that Millie's bedtime is fast approaching.

* * *

Millie sleeps as Harmon drives. A rectangle of corn forms a small break in the thick stand of oaks, hickories, and pines on the right side of the road. Decelerating, he taps his wife on the shoulder.

"Look," he says, pointing to a sign advertising fresh produce. "Farm-farm-farm."

"Oooooh, farm-farm-farm," says Millie, who had run and danced barefoot through a cornfield on their second date. "Corn farm: how wonderful."

Harmon helps Millie out of the car, and they walk hand-in-hand across the grass. At the edge of the field sits a weathered card table shaded by a shagbark hickory, its shavings crunching beneath their shoes as they approach. Sitting on the table is an old cigar box for money and a book for customers to record their purchases. They are alone. Millie ignores the table, heading straight for a bin full of corn. She repeats her mantra, the words *farm* and *corn* filling her with energy. Harmon lets go of her hand, and she goes to work, squeezing an ear, pulling back its husk. She runs her fingers over the kernels to check for freshness. Her body moves with a sense of purpose and dignity. Harmon places his hands on her shoulders and closes his eyes.

They were both 17, when he realized his attraction for the girl whose father had called him a punk. Millie was working a farm stand on the outskirts of Nantasket. It had started to rain. After attending to the last customer, she began to shuck corn, her narrow waist twisting back and forth as she denuded the vegetable. When she saw Harmon looking, she reached into the bin and pulled out an oversized ear. She put it behind her head and pretended to be an Indian—skipping in a circle, chanting, and patting her mouth. Then she gathered a handful of tassels and placed them around her neck, before sashaying behind a stack of unwashed potatoes. He wasn't sure if she were making fun of someone or pretending to be a dancer, but her sense of humor had him hooked.

A car downshifts, causing Harmon to open his eyes. A young couple in an SUV pause briefly before shooting up the hill. When the vehicle disappears, a high-pitched chatter lets Harmon and Millie know they have company.

"Painted bunting," says Millie.

Harmon turns toward the hickory. A moment later, the bird flutters out of the trees, its striking blue head, red-orange breast, and yellow-green wings reminding him of an Indian legend: the Great Spirit was running low on dye and had to use more than one color to finish creating the bird. Perhaps the deity could come up with a similar remedy for a shrinking supply of brain tissue. Millie drops the corn and begins to sigh and bleat. Harmon says a "Hail Mary" as he puts money in the box.

At home Harmon boils the corn—fifteen minutes with a teaspoon of salt—while Millie sits at the kitchen table. Every so often she nods in approval, as if she were back at the high school teaching home economics. When the vegetable has cooled, he uses a sharp knife to cut the kernels into a bowl.

"Very good," says Millie.

Harmon smiles.

Millie pushes away the food. Harmon microwaves a bowl of chicken noodle, hands her a spoon, and she eats. After the dishes are put away, he checks his email. Ferdie1949 is still trying to fix his father's old Philco. The radio works, the customer says, except when it comes to WIRL, the only station his father will listen to.

Harmon suggests "compensating condensers to peak up the signal. Then you can retune the IF coils."

Despite her lack of interest in old radios, Millie had made a point, when Harmon started his business, to learn all the jargon she could get her hands on. When he asked her why, she gave him a look of defiance.

"Just try and stop me," said Millie.

"I wouldn't think of it," replied Harmon.

She had always been smarter than he.

* * *

The sex had long fizzled out, but the couple never stopped flirting, at least not until Millie got sick. A few years ago, she made up a song about radio parts and performed it as a striptease. Harmon wasn't much for music and dance, but Millie's act had made him laugh. He'd do anything to see her perform it again.

He Googles Ferdie's father's radio station and turns up the sound.

"You've been listening to Vaughn Monroe," says the announcer, " 'the voice with hairs on its chest.' "

"Never heard of him," says Harmon, "but I'm sure Millie has." Harmon heads outside to fill the birdfeeders, which were ransacked recently by a family of bears. When he returns, he checks on Millie. She's awake. The radio station has timed out.

"Continental," she says, waving a scarf above her head. "Continental."

"You want to go on a trip?" says Harmon.

"Continental," says Millie, her voice impatient, her face flushed.

"We usually fly Delta, but if you want to go on Continental, that's fine. Where shall we go? Florida?"

"No."

"Back home?"

"No."

The next morning Harmon receives a call from Julie, who has heard a segment on the news and is now worried that Millie might wander into the national forest and get mauled by a bear. He nearly tells her about the feeders but stops himself.

"We're both fine," he says, "as fine as one can expect."

* * *

Millie won't talk. Harmon looks at her throat, which is red. They skip the trip to The Grease in the Pan and head to the doctor, who prescribes antibiotics. Millie has a bug.

At the pharmacy, they run into Betty Lynn, who insists on coming over to help. Harmon hands her a five and asks her to pick up some pastries.

"I think she's been asking for a continental breakfast," says

Harmon, unable to forget Millie's last spoken words.

When Betty Lynn arrives, Millie pushes away the food. The only sounds she makes are bleats and sighs and an occasional cough. Harmon speaks to the doctor, who calls in a cough suppressant. Betty Lynn picks it up. When the narcotic takes effect, Harmon and Betty Lynn sip sweet tea on the screened-in porch.

"I know you don't want to hear this, but you may need to think about some other options," says Betty Lynn, her drawl accompanied by an assortment of chirps and squawks, as the birds compete for a chance at the feeders.

"You're right," says Harmon. "I don't want to hear this."

Betty Lynn pauses. "A nursing home isn't the only option."

"I know, but I can't afford to bring someone in."

"I wouldn't mind . . ."

"No," Harmon interrupts.

"What about Julie?"

"No."

"Why not?"

Harmon groans. "She's got her own life."

"Have you asked her?"

"No, and I'm not about to."

* * *

After Betty Lynn leaves, and the couple go to bed, Harmon dreams that the word *continental* is the key to a puzzle that will cure Millie's disease. A six-letter word converges vertically at the *i*. He thinks for a moment and writes the word *divide*. Suddenly awake, he checks on Millie, who is sleeping soundly. He turns on the computer and goes to the *Oxford English Dictionary*, where he reads about a continental quilt. He tiptoes up to the attic to look through the bin marked *WINTER,* where he retrieves a down duvet they had bought on a trip to England. On his way down the stairs, he stumbles and Millie awakens.

"I've found the continental," says Harmon, placing the bedcovering over his wife.

Millie yawns and pushes away the offering.

Regaining some of her strength, Millie fails to recover her voice. She spends most of her time in bed. Over the upcoming days, Harmon presents her with an assortment of offerings, from the pictures of the family trip across Colorado's continental divide to Julie's old geography project, a papier-mâché model depicting the continental drift. Millie fails to speak. Her appetite wanes. He takes her to the doctor, who recommends a nursing home. Harmon refuses. Back home, he reads about the Continental Congress, continental copper, and continental currency. He falls asleep very late. Before dawn, he's awakened by the sound of whimpering. He switches on the light to see an empty space next to him. He finds Millie crying on the floor of the walk-in closet.

"It's OK," says Harmon, stroking his wife's hair. "It was dark, and you got lost. I could've done the same thing."

Millie bleats, and Harmon helps her back to bed. Once she has fallen asleep, he cries.

The following day Harmon returns to the attic to look for Millie's father's old coin collection.

"Continental currency," he says, placing a German Riechmark in Millie's palm.

When she bites down on the coin, he takes it away, along with the rest of the collection.

After Harmon has administered the cough medicine, Millie sleeps, and he checks his email. Ferdie1949 wants to go with the compensating condensers. As Harmon prepares the order, he tunes his computer to WIRL and listens to Fred Astaire singing *Night and Day*. The announcer reminds listeners that Turner Classic Movies is showing Fred and Ginger in *The Gay Divorcé* at eight.

"Sounds awful," says Harmon.

"Call in now and name a song from *The Gay Divorcé*," says the DJ. "The first caller will receive a $10 gift certificate for any CV Green's Pharmacy."

Harmon clicks on an email update from the Alzheimer's

online support group. Joanna from North Carolina fell and broke her hip. She's in the hospital, and her husband has been moved to an "assisted living facility specializing in memory care." Harmon spoke to her in an online chat last month, after her husband had stuffed a peanut up his nose. Harmon opts out of the email updates and turns up the sound.

"You're on the air," says the DJ.

The caller wins a gift certificate for naming a song called *The Continental.*

Harmon feels his heart skip a beat.

"That's it," he whispers.

A moment later, he calls up Fred and Ginger on YouTube. He watches closely, as the two skitter down a white staircase.

"Too many steps," says Harmon, as the dancers perform their fancy footwork. "Probably make me into a sissy."

* * *

He buys the soundtrack of *The Gay Divorcé,* along with a dance dictionary. Millie completes another round of antibiotics. She still doesn't speak, and her energy is low. They go to The Grease in the Pan. This time Millie eats her hash browns. When she gets home, she throws up. As she sleeps, Harmon watches *The Continental* on YouTube, listens to his new CD, and reads about dance steps. So far he's deciphered Fred's first slow step: a *rond de jambe,* meaning "a circular movement of the leg," followed by some kind of foot drag. He goes to the mirror to try the movement. As he circles his leg from front to side, he loses his balance.

"This is ridiculous."

He reads out his notes: "Front, side, back, side. Step-drag, step-drag."

He tries it again and messes up on the step-drag. "I must be out of my mind."

He concentrates on the lyrics:

It has a passion, The Continental,
An invitation to moonlight and romance.
It's quite the fashion, The Continental,

Because you tell of your love while you dance.

* * *

The following week Harmon teaches himself the first few steps of *The Continental,* and Millie stays mostly in bed. She can no longer walk on her own. Her eating is sporadic and is sometimes followed by violent spells of vomiting. Harmon knows she is dying. He calls Julie, and she books a flight. He stops teaching himself *The Continental.* The night before Julie's arrival, Harmon hears a noise while brushing his teeth. When he comes out of the bathroom, he finds Millie dragging the boom box across the living room floor. Harmon bends down, and Millie mewls. Her expression is one of desperation, her sunken eye sockets quivering and dripping with tears.

"You want to dance?" he says.

Millie fails to respond. Her face is stiff.

Harmon turns on the music and helps his wife to a standing position. They barely move, husband holding wife by the waist and hand, as Ginger Rogers sings of "two bodies swaying." Millie turns toward Harmon, and he kisses her cheek. They begin to dance.

About the Author

photo by: Franklin Diaz

Dr. Kendall Klym has won numerous awards for his short stories, which have been published in literary journals including *Puerto del Sol, Hunger Mountain,* and the *Tampa Review*. Klym is a three-time honorable mention winner of the Great American Fiction Contest, sponsored by the *Saturday Evening Post*. In 2017, he was awarded a two-month fellowship at the Fairhope Center for the Writing Arts, where he completed the first draft of *The Man with an Amber Halo,* a novel of grief and redemption based on the sudden death of his partner. He completed the second draft upon the completion of a Monson Arts Residency in November of 2018. A former professional ballet dancer and newspaper journalist, Klym incorporates elements of dance and journalism in his writing. He holds a Ph.D. in English, with a concentration in Fiction Writing, from the University of Wales, Aberystwyth, and taught creative writing, composition, and literature full time at Kennesaw State University from 2011-18.